TWISTED SINNER

A DARK ROMANCE

CARA BIANCHI

Copyright © 2022 - Cara Bianchi

Cover © 2022 - @covers_by_wonderland (Instagram)

All rights reserved.

No part of this book may be reproduced in any form or by any electronic or mechanical means, including information storage and retrieval systems, without written permission from the author, except for the use of brief quotations in a book review.

TRIGGER WARNINGS

It's my responsibility as an author to be clear about any possible triggers in this book. Your safety and mental health are very important, so please don't read this story if you may be adversely affected by the following:

- **graphic and extensive descriptions of sexual acts** (consent is dubious in at least one instance)

- **blood kink and knife play** (for real - our leading man, in particular, is a big fan)

- **forced orgasms** and edging

- **praise kink**

- **sexually-charged physical violence**, including slapping, pinching, biting, and the 'hand necklace'

- **other violence**, specifically shooting and stabbing

- **murder** (not sadistic or prolonged)

- **peril involving a young child**, both on the page and in description. This does not include sexual or other abuse but may cause distress to some readers

- depictions of **Post-Traumatic Stress Disorder**, including flashbacks and panic attacks

- **suicide** and **suicide** ideation (not depicted)

- **mentions of pedophilia, child abuse, and human trafficking** (not on the page or described)

- **alcohol** consumption depicted on the page. References made to drugs but not descriptively

A quick word on consent and safety in relationships:

This book and the characters depicted herein are in no way intended to represent safe or healthy relationship dynamics, particularly how they handle their kinks.

If you are interested in exploring any of the practices described in this story, please don't use my book as a primer! I encourage you to do you own research and put your physical and psychological safety first.

Thank you and be safe!

If you're all good, carry on, you beautiful sicko.

For all my freaks who like their men just a bit unhinged. I unlocked all new kinks when I wrote this book, and my husband is deeply, profoundly afraid of me now.

CONTENTS

CHAPTER 1	1
Ali	1
Leo	7
CHAPTER 2	13
Leo	13
CHAPTER 3	22
Ali	22
CHAPTER 4	29
Ali	29
CHAPTER 5	42
Leo	42
CHAPTER 6	51
Leo	51
CHAPTER 7	58
Ali	58
CHAPTER 8	71
Ali	71
Leo	73
Ali	81
CHAPTER 9	84
Ali	84
Leo	89
CHAPTER 10	93
Ali	93
CHAPTER 11	102
Leo	102

CHAPTER 12	110
Ali	110
Leo	115
CHAPTER 13	118
Leo	118
CHAPTER 14	127
Ali	127
CHAPTER 15	136
Ali	136
Leo	138
Ali	142
CHAPTER 16	146
Leo	146
CHAPTER 17	154
One hour later...	154
Leo	154
Ali	159
CHAPTER 18	164
Ali	164
CHAPTER 19	171
Leo	171
Ali	176
CHAPTER 20	178
Ali	178
Leo	179
CHAPTER 21	184
Ali	184
Leo	188
Ali	190
CHAPTER 22	193
Leo	193
CHAPTER 23	203
One hour later...	203

Ali	203
Leo	206
Ali	209
CHAPTER 24	215
Four hours later...	215
Leo	215
Ali	218
CHAPTER 25	222
Leo	222
Ali	226
CHAPTER 26	231
Two hours later...	231
Ali	231
Leo	244
CHAPTER 27	248
One week later...	248
Leo	248
Ali	251
Epilogue	257
Mailing List	279
Also by Cara Bianchi	281

1

Ali

I want to kill every fucker in this room.

The whole place is packed with absolute assholes. Businessmen, lawyers, judges, politicians, and police. Corrupt, power-hungry garbage people.

The women are purely ornamental. Dripping in jewels, this season's best pieces hanging off their bodies. No amount of makeup can completely hide the hollows under their eyes, though. It takes wealth to be into both couture *and* cocaine.

No one pays me any mind as I slink through the crowd. I pick up a flute from a passing tray and sip the fizz. *Not bad.*

Senator Coffey knows everyone in this city who's worth knowing. In his circles, it's seen as poor form to need to be introduced to anyone. It makes it look like you're not connected.

I use this to my advantage and smile now and again, waggling my fingers in an affectatious little wave. The guests who catch my eye respond in kind, assuming I'm someone's young trophy wife.

None of these people understand what it's like to be me.

The dress I'm wearing has some serious miles on it. It's the only one I own that looks the part, and I'm walking the line between 'vintage' and 'old and shitty.' It looks much better since my nimble-fingered roomie Roxy put the split in it. A flash of my long leg draws the eye away from the fraying straps.

I tuck my hand into my purse, touching the key card for the hundredth time.

The senator is more careful than his wife. He's the one with all the security, but she's wandering around on her own, and it was appallingly easy to get his room key from her - the dizzy bitch didn't suspect a thing. She hasn't noticed it's gone in the half-hour I've been tailing her.

The only problem is I don't know which room it's for. The cards are all blank, sensibly enough.

Time to move.

I shake my hair loose, ruffling it a little. I've been practicing my drunk walk, and I have it just right. Kicking my shoe loose, I wobble awkwardly out of the function room and across to the front desk, where the concierge is at his post.

"Shcuse me," I slur, looking at his name badge. "Hal, right? So I'm s'posed to go see *Adrian*," I drop my voice to a whisper and giggle, "I mean *Senator Coffey*. He gave me the key and asked me to wait up there for him, but I had too many fizzies." I hiccup, and the man smiles, his eyes flashing up and down my body. "He told me the room number, but I forgot. Help a girl out?"

Hal leans forward over the desk and smiles.

His breath has the sulfurous tang of gingivitis. I wonder how he even got a job here when his aesthetic is 'pocket masturbator.'

"I understand. Give me a quick look, and I'll let you go about your day."

Prick. Of course he wants something that's not his to take. Don't they all?

My lifestyle doesn't allow me to fly the flag for feminism. Back when I had some principles, all they ever got me was trouble, so I learned to take shortcuts where I could.

Tucking a thumb into my decolletage, I pull the neckline lower as I bend over, giving the concierge a good view of my full tits.

"Perfection. I'm sure the senator will have a great time with you." He flashes a charmless smile. "It's suite ten, top floor. Would you like me to let him know you're here?"

I place my finger over my lips. "Shhh, Hal. He already knows. Just keep Mrs. Coffey down here. She and the Police Commissioner's wife are yumming up cocktail blinis right now, so it's unlikely, but you never know."

"My lips are sealed, sweetpea."

I shudder as I head for the elevator.

Picking pockets is my day job, not bullshit like this.

It's okay, Ali. You're almost there. It'll be worth it.

The floor is deserted. You'd think a man like the senator would have his room guarded, but he's more worried about himself and too cheap to hire enough men. Good job he's well-known to have a penchant for call girls.

The key card works the first time, the lock emitting a low beep as it clicks open. I slide the card into the slot in the wall, activate the lights, and lock the door behind me.

As I expected, the safe is in the closet. Same as ninety-nine times out of a hundred so I don't waste time looking elsewhere.

In my experience, hotel safes open with a swipe of the room key. The numbered dial in front of me is not ideal.

"Shit," I mutter.

Heavy steps outside make me freeze.

The room isn't a fortress. There's nowhere to hide. I could shimmy along the ledge and get to another balcony - it wouldn't be the first time I've done something like that - but that's a pretty risky approach. The last time I had to escape from a hotel window, I made it to the ground, but I sprained my ankle so badly that I was on my ass for two weeks. I can't risk that happening again. Roxy had to pick up the slack, and I worried about her getting hurt out there.

The footsteps pass. I close my eyes and steady myself, counting aloud under my breath.

"One Mississippi, two Mississippi..."

The band starts up downstairs, playing Motown.

I make it to forty before the blood stops rushing in my ears. *Back to the safe.*

Hotel safes have a built-in override code. The hotel should change it, but they rarely do. This happens when a concierge is too busy being a bad-breathed pussy hound instead of doing his job.

I type in the standard code. *1-1-1-1.*

A little red light and I'm denied.

Okay. No worries. Try again.

0-0-0-0.

Bzzzz. The light turns green, and the safe door swings open.

Right there before me is what I'm after.

My heart skips a beat with sheer relief. I never thought I'd have it in my hands again.

I swing my dress over my hip, revealing my garter holster. I tuck the precious cargo into the pocket beside my blade.

"Thanks, Hal-itosis," I say aloud.

I abandon my wig down the laundry chute outside the room, and I'm out and back downstairs in less than two minutes. I do my sober walk, and with my imperious, posh-bitch face on, Hal doesn't recognize me. I head for the front door and freedom.

Then I see them.

Several men in the same security uniform as the man by the lift. They're outside, and although I can't hear their conversation, I can see well enough through the glass. They're arguing with each other as they load guns.

Oh *fuck*.

I wheel around and head back to the party, trying to figure out what to do. Most people in the room are on the dance floor. I dither awkwardly at the edge, panic seizing me as I hear the security guards in the lobby.

The function room has a door on the other side, with a glowing 'Fire Exit' sign above it. I can't believe I didn't notice before.

The door opens, and a man walks through it. A stupidly gorgeous man. His hair is a dirty blonde, short at the sides but artfully disheveled on top, making me wonder if he wakes up that way.

I'd fucking *love* to find out.

His sea-green eyes scan the room, but when they stop on me, he gives a lop-sided grin, revealing dimples in his stubble. I didn't think anyone could look that good in real life.

He moves with a lion's easy gait, removing his jacket as he walks my way. Without breaking stride, he throws it on the ground between two tables and picks up another randomly from the back of a chair. I see the muscles in his arms as he lifts them, pulling the jacket over his body.

I should move. Why am I just *standing* here like a moron? The doors are gonna crash open any second, and those security guys will drag me out of here...

The man seems to cover the last few feet in an instant. He takes my waist in both his hands and pulls me toward him, and I lose my footing, falling into him. Instinctively, I put my hands on his chest to steady myself.

He walks me sideways, the revelers moving to accommodate us.

"What the *fuck* are you doing?" I hiss. "Let me go!"

"No way, *tigritsa*. Move your beautiful ass, or I drop you on it. Your call."

The man grabs my hand, lacing his fingers through mine. I try, but I can't get free of his grip. He thrusts his arm to one side, taking mine with it. He leans to my ear to speak, his voice velvet smooth.

"Dance."

∼

Ten minutes earlier...

Leo

If other people were as punctual as me, my job would be far easier.

The band was due to start five minutes ago, but they're still tuning up. I can't proceed until they play because I need the sound for cover.

Five minutes isn't much for most people, but to me, it can be the difference between success and failure.

Not that I've ever *actually* failed. Made a mess, maybe. But I always achieve the original objective.

Judge Brazier has finally been lured out of hiding to attend the senator's fundraiser. The fat fuck presumably thought a free bar and buffet was worth risking his life, but we have standards, and reneging on a promise is not something that the Gurin Bratva can forgive.

Pavel Gurin sends *me* to work when there's no forgiveness, negotiation, or way back. When there's nothing left to do but end someone.

I look through my rifle sight at the hotel balcony. It's taking that hooker a fuck of a long time to blow the judge. Who knew the old bastard had that kind of self-control? Still, she's probably wondering what I'm playing at. I paid her a considerable sum to keep him there until I disposed of him.

There are many things I'd rather do on a Saturday night than sit on a church roof in the blistering cold and watch a soon-to-be-dead lawman get head.

As if on cue, my cell phone vibrates in my pocket. I double-tap my earbud.

"*Dobryy vecher*, Benedikt."

"How's it going, *tovarishch*?" Ben asks.

"I'm perched on top of Saint Michael's like a fucking gargoyle, waiting for the music to start so I can get this done and go home. Other than that, it's magical."

"Well, don't wait too long. Brazier fucked us over badly. If he hadn't sent our boys down, we'd still have control of the New Jersey operation, and the bastard won't even take our fucking calls?"

"This happens when Pavel plays politics."

I see Brazier pushing the girl away from him and turning towards the balcony door.

Shit.

"Gotta go," I say, hanging up.

With my years of muscle memory at the helm, I only need a nanosecond to steady the sight.

I look through the scope at the porky bastard who screwed us over.

Fuck it. This guy is dying *now*. I'll busk it from there.

With the silencer, the shot is not as loud as it could be, but it's loud enough. On the street below, the hotel doorman looks up.

Brazier's expression doesn't change, but in the center of his chest, a bloom of red stains his shirt. The hooker covers her face with her hands and scuttles to one side, anticipating him falling. Brazier looks stupidly at his feet for a moment, frowning as if they're to blame somehow, before keeling over, his forehead smashing off the railing.

Part of me wanted to see him fall off the balcony. That would have been spectacular. But no, he's in a heap, his legs halfway into his room, blood pooling beneath him. The girl jumps over him, carefully avoiding the blood, and leaves, closing the hotel room door behind her.

The band starts up.

Typical.

I leave the rifle where it is, for now, only laying it and its stand down and out of sight. The tower isn't too high, and it's an easy two-minute maneuver to abseil down on the side that faces into the churchyard. With my feet on solid ground, all I have to do is walk through the gate and onto the street.

I take off my gloves and put them in a trash can as I survey the scene over the road.

The security guys are trying to work out what to do. One appears to be calling the police, but the others are fanning out in small groups. Some are surrounding the building while others move into the streets. They know *something* has happened.

Whatever I do now, I'd better do it quickly.

I walk toward the hotel, keeping my stride brisk, and duck down the alley to the right of the building. I see the fire exit propped open.

Is it stupid to sneak into the party where I murdered a guest? Probably. But doing sensible things isn't how I got my reputation. I got it for killing people for the Bratva and doing it efficiently every time.

As I push the door open, I see people dancing. I look around for threats, but my eyes stop moving when they alight on the vision before me.

Sweet fucking Jesus and all the saints.

How she can be here alone, I have no idea. But the sight of her is heating me up in more ways than one.

The woman's dress was once a piece of high-end evening wear , but it looks a little careworn. Not that it matters. She fills it out perfectly, a toned leg visible through the split in the black satin. Her cleavage is deep and inviting; below, a tiny waist kicks out into curvy hips. A shiny blue-black bob frames her face, with straight bangs drawing attention to almond-shaped gray eyes.

My feet carry me toward her. I'm vaguely aware of shucking off my jacket and picking up another - a superficial field disguise and instinctive by now - but I can't take my eyes off her face.

She's staring at me. I have that effect sometimes.

Very few people know who I am, but many think they do. That's because I'm often seen but never placed. A ghost, a rumor.

And that's how I like it.

I take the woman's waist in my hands, fascinated by her lack of resistance.

Oh yeah. You can get me warm, baby.

It's not until we're on the dancefloor that she comes out of her trance, but despite her protestations, I'm not letting go.

"Dance," I say, holding her hand out to the side in the classic pose.

I wheel her around, and she has no choice but to follow my movements if she wants to stay on her feet. The hand on my chest clenches into a claw, her nails digging into me.

"I don't want to fucking dance!"

The song ends, and we stop moving, but I don't let her go. Her hand leaves my chest and reaches for the split in her dress.

I catch her by the wrist and place her hand on my shoulder.

"Hold on," I murmur.

Security guards enter the room through both doors. There aren't many, but they look pissed.

The band starts up again, playing a slow number.

The woman suddenly closes the small space between us, pressing her body to mine.

"I'm Ali."

2

Leo

Ali molds herself to me, resting her cheek on my chest. I respond in kind, enjoying the feel of her body against mine.

"It's great to not quite meet you," I say, "but I'm sure we can get to know each other."

She's lively in my hands, her hips undulating as she sways to the music. My cock stirs as I tighten my hold on her waist, grinding against her a little. She slips her fingers onto the back of my neck, raking gently with her nails, and I can't suppress a low groan.

Only I could go from borderline hypothermic five minutes ago to on fire in the arms of some feisty little minx. Specifically, the one who is now practically humping my thigh in the middle of the dancefloor at a party I wasn't invited to.

I drag my eyes away from her face to look at the security guards. They haven't spotted me. They don't know who or what they're looking for, anyway.

When I glance at Ali, her eyes are wide and darting. Her fingers on my neck grip involuntarily, and despite the danger, my mind's eye is filled with the image of my hand wrapped around her slender throat.

Her stormy eyes are full of *something*. I'm not sure what it is. Fear, definitely, but not fear of *me*. Whatever it is, adrenaline gets this girl going. I'm pretty sure her pussy is acting out right now, and if I can extract myself from this situation in one piece, maybe I'll help her out. As a favor to her, of course.

"What's up, baby?" I ask. "You need something?"

She wrenches her hand from mine and reaches for my waistband.

"Kiss me," she whispers.

I lower my face to hers, catching her scent as I get closer. It's fresh and heady, bergamot and rose emanating from her neckline. Her lips are pillowy soft, and as they meet mine, she's surprisingly coy, yielding to my tongue.

I'm not usually the kissing type. I'd rather move on to the main event than waste time on the details. But this is fucking sublime.

Now that she's over her initial shyness, her kisses are getting hungrier. Her hand is inside my pants, but she can't get to my cock without someone noticing, so she runs her fingers through the trail of hair leading down to where she wants to be.

I grab her ass with both hands. It's bigger than I would have expected, but there's no way I'm complaining. She catches my lower lip in her teeth and bites hard enough to hurt.

"Ouch," I say. I run my tongue over the sore spot and taste the unmistakable coppery tinge where she split my skin. "Aren't you gonna at least buy me a drink first?"

"Come with me to the bathroom," she says, nodding at the padded door beside the bar.

I look around. The security guys are leaving the room, but even if I wanted to, now would be a bad time to make my escape.

And I sure as hell *don't* want to escape. I'm hyped up from the action and this angel is driving me fucking crazy. I didn't expect to meet a gorgeous woman and rail her in a hotel bathroom, but if there's one thing I'm good at, it's taking opportunities when they appear.

"Lead on," I say, squeezing Ali's ass. She removes her hand from my pants and walks away.

For a second, I think she's leaving. I'm about to go after her and drag the little prick-tease in there myself when she looks over her shoulder, beckoning me with her eyes. She walks into the bathroom, and I follow.

I'm only a few seconds behind her, but I nearly lose my mind when I enter the room.

Ali is perched on the counter between the two basins with the mirrored wall behind. Her knees are up in front of her, slightly parted, and her dress is pulled up to her waist. Despite her legs in the way, my view isn't totally impeded, and between her feet, I can see her plump pussy lips spilling over the thin fabric of her G-string.

I close the door and lean against it.

"You're a fucking nasty little tease," I say as I move toward her. "Anyone ever told you that before?"

"No," she says.

"Good." I put my hands on her knees and push them apart.

The aroma of her arousal is incredible, but the sight is even better. The lights are low, but her inner thighs still shimmer with her wetness.

I knew this girl wanted to play, but I didn't realize she was this turned on.

I step forward, standing between her legs, my hands sliding up along her body. I move my palm along the split in her dress and find something I didn't expect.

I pull the blade free from the sheath. It's a short but sturdy dagger in the style of a hunting knife - not the kind I carry, but a good all-rounder. I turn it in my hand as Ali leans back on her hands.

"So I guess your purse isn't big enough for this?"

She has the grace to look embarrassed. "It's for protection," she says. Her eyes move from the knife to my face and back again.

I press the flat of the blade's tip against her abdomen.

"Protection from *what*?" I murmur.

Her breath catches, but she holds my gaze.

"Scarier men than *you*," she says, her tone icy.

This woman has nerves of steel. I'm surprised at how much her complete lack of fear is turning me on right now. I'm so hard it's painful.

I tuck the blade under the G-string, just beside her hipbone, and cut through it. I do the same to the other side, and with a quick flick, the flimsy panties are gone.

"I'm gonna eat this pussy until you come. That's what you want, right?"

I bend down, breathing over her mound. She moans quietly before grabbing my hair and pushing my face into her. Her other hand taps my shoulder.

"Give me my knife back. *Now*."

I toss it behind me, and it clatters loudly against the marble tile wall.

"I'm not going to give it back to you, *tigritsa*. I want to keep my spinal column intact. Besides, I don't perform well under threat of death."

That's a lie. I do my best work when I think I might get killed. But I don't care why Ali has a knife. A woman who wears an evening dress and a garter holster is beyond my experience, and I'm down for anything.

I ignore Ali's irritable snarl and run my tongue through her slit. The burgeoning complaint is replaced with a shuddery breath.

"Ohhh," she sighs, opening her legs wider. Her clit stands proud, begging for touch. She pulls my hair as I lap at her little button.

Dear God, she has a pretty pussy. A trimmed patch of downy hair crowns her sex, which is flushed and rosy, dewy with her juice.

She's ready for me. But I've barely begun.

I slip a finger into her, and she bucks her hips, squeezing it with her internal muscles. If she can grip my finger that tightly, she's going to feel amazing on my cock. I'm struck by the urge to see those stunning tits, and I remove my hand from her inner thigh to reach up her body.

"Pull this down."

Ali's hips roll against my mouth.

"No," she says, pushing my hand away. "Someone might come in."

"So?" I slow my movements so I can speak, and she groans in frustration. "If someone comes through that door now, they'll see you fucking my face. I don't see how your tits being covered will make any difference. And *I* wouldn't give a shit if I was balls-deep inside you and your fucking *father* walked in."

I add a second finger, sliding them slowly in and out of her. She moves to meet me, trying to wring out every bit of sensation, but it's not enough, and we both know it.

"Ali, I'm not asking. Show your body to me."

With an exasperated grunt, she nudges the straps off her shoulders, and her tits are naked before me. She looks so slutty with nothing more than a bundle of satin at her waist, her golden skin on show for me. Her nipples are large and hard; the same deep rose as her pussy lips. Impossible to ignore.

I stop licking her pussy and slap her hand away from my head. She reaches for my hair again, trying to wrap her long legs around my shoulders.

"No, you can't just—"

"I can. Like I said, it's not up to you." I move up her body and take her nipple between my lips. She's distracted enough for me to grab her wrists and pin them to the counter as I bite the hot little peak.

"Oh, you fucking bastard."

I press my erection against her naked pussy, her wetness soaking into my pants. The urge to free my cock and plunge into her is almost overwhelming, but I resist because something about her makes me want to please and deny her simultaneously. She's so vital, so alive in my hands, desperately fighting to get what she wants.

It's the hottest thing I've ever fucking known, and I don't want this to end.

With some effort, I stop grinding against her and return my tongue to her pussy. I release one of her hands so I can touch her, and as my fingers slip into her, I realize that she's close. Her muscles are spasming crazily, clutching at my fingers and trying to pull them deeper.

"Ask nicely, and I'll let you come."

I leave my fingers inside her and stand up so she can see my face. Ali opens her eyes and looks at me.

"What?"

I rub her clit with my thumb, and her lips part with a breathy moan.

"You heard me." I enjoy her fury as she sees that I'm serious. "Ask me to let you come."

"No."

This woman has bigger balls than I do. There's no way she's getting away with it.

"You keep refusing, and I swear, I'll walk out of here and leave you with your self-respect as shredded as your panties."

"You egotistic asshole..."

"Yeah, yeah. I've heard all this shit before, but it makes no fucking difference. You just lost your asking privileges, *tigritsa*." I move my thumb rhythmically, feeling her tense up around my fingers. I curl them a little, finding the sweet spot, and she grits her teeth.

"You want me to make it happen for you?" I stop touching her clit, resting the pad of my thumb beside it. "Then you can fucking *beg*."

Ali can't take any more. With a scream of rage, she grips the counter's edge with her free hand and nearly slides off completely in her effort to push onto my hand.

"Please!" she cries. "Please make me come!"

Twisted Sinner 21

I ramp up my movements again, enjoying her expression as her eyes roll. Her mouth falls open, and I imagine shoving my cock down her throat until she chokes.

"Since you didn't ask," I say, working her clit, "my name is Leo. Use my name when you're begging. Who am I?"

"Leo!" I feel her pussy surge, getting wetter around my fingers. "I'm begging *you*, Leo. Don't stop now. Let me come, please!"

"That's my good girl."

I give a final firm thrust as she slaps her hand over her mouth, stifling her scream as she comes all over my hand. She quivers and whimpers, and I remove my fingers from her pussy and raise my hand to her face.

"Open your mouth."

Ali does what she's told immediately, and then I know for sure. She's a polecat, a wicked little vixen, but she wants to be a good girl. *My* good girl.

I stick my fingers in her mouth, sliding them over her tongue. She sucks at her wetness, and my cock tingles at the feeling. I slip my fingertips to the back of her throat, a deep growl escaping me as she gags. I remove my hand, and she grins at me before pushing me away gently with her foot.

I'm already undoing my zipper as she gets to her feet. She moves toward and past me, opening the bathroom door to peek out.

"Everybody's gone."

I look past her and through the gap. Some guests linger, but the room is almost empty. I never even noticed the music

3

Ali

I know it's cruel. But once I come down from my orgasm, I remember what I was doing before this fine-as-all-fuck man snatched hold of me. I decide he can wait for his turn.

"Are you coming?" I ask, looking over my shoulder at Leo.

"Apparently not," he replies, doing up his zipper. "Never let a good deed go unpunished, right?"

We duck out of the bathroom, and without a word, he takes my hand. We lapse into a leisurely stroll as though we have every right to be here.

As we enter the lobby, I glance nervously at the desk, but stinky Hal is nowhere to be seen. A lone security guard is standing beside the front door, and through the glass, I can see flashing blue lights. I squeeze Leo's hand so hard that he looks at me.

"What's the matter?" he asks.

"Nothing. It's just—"

"Stop." The security guard's hand grabs my upper arm. "I didn't see you at the party. Are you a guest here or—"

Leo steps in front of me and shoves the guard in the chest. He lets go of me and stumbles.

"What the fuck?"

Leo doesn't give him a chance to get the upper hand. As the guard regains his footing, Leo's right in his face.

"She's with *me*," he says, "and that means you're manhandling something that doesn't fucking belong to you. Anything to say?"

The security guard looks confused. He'd be well within his rights if he got us both arrested, but he can see something in Leo's face that unsettles him.

"Sorry?" the guard asks, sounding unsure.

"You should be. Say it to *her*."

Leo nods at me. The guard looks like he wants to argue, but he doesn't.

"I apologize, miss."

There's an uncomfortable silence.

"What's going on out there?" Leo asks, gesturing at the door onto the street. "Looks like bad news."

The guard looks at Leo like he's grown another head. I can see why. Leo was ready to fuck him up just moments ago, and now, he may as well be asking about the weather.

"A guest got shot," the guard says. "A judge. These things

happen sometimes, but it's scary for the patrons, and the hotel management isn't happy either." He rubs his beard with his fingertips, avoiding Leo's eyes. "I gotta ask, sir. Are you staying at the hotel or attending the party?"

"Neither. But I'll level with you." Leo leans in closer to the guard, sliding his arm around my waist as he does so. "*I* shot him."

The guard bursts into laughter. "Okay, buddy. You go on out there and let the cops know all about it!"

Leo pushes the door open.

It's mayhem out here. Lights flashing, police wrapping crime scene tape around hastily erected barrier posts. No one pays us any mind as we join a small crowd of people being ushered away by a couple of uniformed officers.

"Nothing to see! Keep moving. Come on! Get away from the area, people!"

The group scatters as we reach the end of the street, and I turn back to take in the scene.

Cop cars, security officers, police. A helicopter shines a beacon of light over the churchyard and streets beyond.

"If you *had* shot the guy, you'd be fucked," I say.

"I'd *love* to be fucked, Ali," he replies, flashing me a grin, "but I guess we've started this all backward. Drink?"

The basement bar is a wonderful little dive. It's one of those places with a certain gentrified grubbiness - all bare brick walls and rough floorboards, with bar prices that guarantee the likes of me could never afford to actually get drunk. But I love a Whiskey Highball, and it's incredible to have one made from *good* whiskey rather than the stuff I'm usually reduced to.

I sip my drink and smile.

"Good?" Leo asks.

"Yep. I usually drink Bell's, so this is amazing."

Leo snorts. "Bell's whiskey is a fucking travesty unless you're going to mix it with a lot of coke. *Both* kinds of coke. If your face is numb enough, you won't be able to taste it."

I laugh. "Do you think I can afford cocaine if I drink Bell's?"

"Cocaine is filth, *tigritsa*. But I wouldn't serve that shit at my worst enemy's wake." He nods at my glass. "And if you're a Highball girl, it's even more important that it goes down smooth and hits the spot."

I catch the twinkle in his eye and feel myself flush.

Yeah, I get it, you arrogant bastard. You made me beg for my climax, and when you praised me for it, I came like never before.

I cough and cross my legs. "So, do you live in the city?"

Leo shakes his head. "I'm back and forth for work, so I know it well, but no. I don't call anywhere home."

He's a rolling stone, then. Suits me.

"Sounds kinda lonely."

He raises his eyebrows at me. "I'm not lonely now, am I? What about you?"

"I'm a thief," I say.

I don't know why I told him the truth. But he used my own knife to cut away my panties, so he must already have *some* idea that my lifestyle is kinda shady.

Leo smiles and touches his wristwatch. "Phew," he says with a grin, "it's still there. Don't take this, please. It has sentimental value." He finishes his beer. "What's the appeal of the light-fingered life, then? Surely you get caught all the time."

"I do. But I have to eat."

"You must have a rap sheet a mile long. Is your name *really* Ali, or did you change it?"

"It's Alina. For my surname, I use Green. It's nicely generic and the first one I thought of when an angry cop asked me."

I watch as he draws a waitress to him with just a smile and a nod. She glides over as if he's magnetic, and I suppress a frisson of jealousy.

Does he do shit like this all the time? I kind of used *him*, sure, but I'll admit to some hypocrisy.

I want to believe he never saw a vision of loveliness like me before. But *look* at him. He could trip and fall into a willing vagina.

The waitress has rearranged her bangs several times already in the five seconds she's been interacting with him. He orders another beer, and she dashes off to get it, probably powered by her red-hot cooch. He looks at me and breaks into laughter, and I realize my displeasure must be writ large on my face.

"She's getting me a drink, baby," he says. "No need to get your panties in a bunch. Oh no, wait..."

He had to remind me of my underwear-free state. I check my dress isn't riding up and take a big gulp of my whiskey, the burn pleasant on my throat.

He gives me an idiotic grin, and I laugh despite myself.

I *need* to fuck this guy.

Just the way he's lounging like he owns the place is intimidating every man in here. And every woman who spots him is wearing that glazed, slack-jawed expression we get when we want to hop on a dick.

I hope he has somewhere we can go because Roxy and I have a no-men-at-home rule, for safety. And this guy is definitely *not* safe. There's something in his lips, his hands, and his eyes that just screams bad news.

I'm pretty sure he's not interested in telling me anything about his life because he's not looking for anything serious. Just a one-time thing, and tomorrow he'll go on his way and leave me with happy memories and a very sore kitty. At least, here's hoping because the whiskey is hitting, and the prospect of him filling me up is very tempting indeed.

"Why did you grab me on the dance floor?" I ask.

"Because you looked so fucking hot that my brain went on the fritz."

The waitress puts the beer down on the table, and he rewards her with a wink. She avoids my eyes as she turns away.

"You told that security guy off for manhandling me after you did practically the same thing. It's not the most sophisticated way to get a lady's attention, is it?"

He shrugs. "Not at all. But I didn't want a *lady's* attention. I wanted yours."

You cheeky fucking...

He sees my anger and wags a finger at me. "Now, now. Don't get that way. You're the one who dragged *me* to the bathroom and rode my face."

"Shh!" I hiss. "The music isn't that loud here. Someone will hear you."

He slides along the bench until his firm thigh is pressed to mine.

"I already heard you," he says, his lips brushing my ear. "You begged me to make you come. I wanna make you say it again."

His hand steals beneath the table and between my legs.

This dress seems to have been designed for easy access. If I sat on Leo's lap, I could ride him right here and get away with it.

His fingertips graze my slit.

"Let's get a cab," he says.

4

Ali

We don't speak in the car. The driver tries to get Leo to talk to him, but after a few grunts, he stops responding, and all is silence.

I know Leo's type. His attractiveness doesn't mask the man he is. They are all the same.

It doesn't matter how much they claim to love you. They all think the world - or specifically, the *women* of the world - owe them something. *Everything*, in fact.

I take the initiative because it's less of a sting when I get dropped on my ass. If I keep my guard up, no one can hurt me. Or, at least, not as much.

When I was little, I was always drawing pictures of wedding dresses. Sighing over Disney movies, dreaming I was the princess.

Yeah, right.

The Disney character I most resemble is Aladdin. A street rat with no prospects, and unlike him, I have neither love nor magic to bail me out.

I have Roxy. But she's so vulnerable, so painfully young. She's sixteen, so I only have four years on her, but she seems childlike in many ways. She kept her hope and faith in people, whereas mine was ripped away over a decade ago.

I went from a cheerful, happy-go-lucky child to an empty shell. When I started speaking again, there was no one left to talk to. Before then, I never knew loneliness like that existed.

Taking care of Roxy keeps me sane and gives me something to hold on to. But it's a vicious circle. I do whatever is necessary to keep her off the streets, so my rap sheet gets longer and longer. Desperation doesn't leave space for meticulous planning, and although I get away more than I get caught, my record prevents me from getting a steady job.

I lean against the seat and close my eyes.

One night.

I can have that, right? A few stolen hours where I can pretend to be someone else, not trapped in this degrading holding pattern.

Crime, payment, poverty, more crime. Some life. My parents would be ashamed of me.

The cab pulls to a halt in front of a pleasant-looking family home. We get out of the cab, and Leo hands several crumpled bills to the driver.

"Who was your fare again?" he asks.

The driver looks confused for a second before the penny drops. "Ah. Yeah. A middle-aged couple from upstate. They were arguing. Never seen them before."

"That's right. Remember, if anyone asks - that's your story. Don't fucking think of rewriting the script, either. I have ways of finding out."

The driver pales and winds up his window, pulling away into the night.

As I watch, Leo sets off down the street.

"Hey!" I point at the house in front of me. "Aren't we going in?"

"Not in *there*, no. Now come on."

~

My palace for the night is a boarded-up bungalow on the edge of a suburb. It reminds me of the Granville place in *It's a Wonderful Life*, the bit where Mary and George throw rocks at the windows and make wishes.

"So this is festive," I say. "If you're planning to murder me, it's very sporting of you to drop such a heavy hint."

"I'm a few weeks late for Halloween."

A sign on the chain-link fence reads, 'Unstable and insecure. Do not cross.'

"Does that refer to you?" I ask.

Leo's face is half in shadow. He looks like he's wearing a mask, and a flash of clarity hits me.

I know *nothing* about this guy. Where the hell has he brought me?

"You mean the sign?" Leo wrinkles his nose. "Nah. I'm not insecure."

I can't help but notice that he doesn't deny the rest. Leo unlocks the front door and pushes it open, beckoning me inside.

Ah well. I'm here now. If he's going to kill me, I hope he fucks me first.

That's a twisted thing to think. *What the hell is wrong with me?*

Leo turns on a light, and I'm shocked to find myself in a beautiful room. It's a lounge, but there's a king-size bed shoved up beneath the mantlepiece. He has a heavy writer's desk, a laptop, and many books in stacks around the room. A thick rug covers most of the floor, but I can see the bare boards beneath. The boarded windows are covered with thick drapes, but when I look closely, I can see that one of the windows is blocked with a shutter rather than a permanent covering.

"Do you live here? You're the best-dressed bum I ever met."

"This is my base. The house used to belong to an associate of mine, but it went to ruin when he passed away. I don't like hotels, so I made it my own."

"I like it." I glance into the hallway. "Anything else to see?"

"Ali, for fuck's sake." Leo puts his hand on the back of my neck, pressing his thumb on my jaw. "I'm not a realtor, okay? This isn't an open house. I never brought anyone here before. But I need privacy for what I want to do, and this is the only place I know I can get that."

I eyeball him warily. "And *what* are you going to do exactly?"

"You owe me something," he says, "and I'm gonna take it."

His hand lashes out, wrapping my wrist like a whip, and he spins me so I'm facing away from him. His fingers on my neck steal around to the front, and he digs the tips into my throat as his lips touch my shoulder.

I'm too surprised to react. Leo is still gripping my wrist, holding my hand to my side, but my other hand is hanging there stupidly at the end of my arm, doing nothing while a total stranger squeezes my neck.

"You think you have hard edges?" he murmurs. He bites my tender flesh hard enough to draw a yelp of shock from me. "You have no idea how soft you can be, *tigritsa*. I know you want to play the bad girl, but you know what *I* want, don't you?"

I'm no longer paralyzed, and my free hand pulls at him, trying to get him to let go of my neck.

"No," I say.

"No *what*?" Leo pushes me, walking me in front of him toward the bed. "You don't know what I want?"

"Don't hurt me," I whisper.

Leo lets go of my neck, and although I'm kinda relieved, I'm also fascinated. He did what I asked, but I'm somehow disappointed. Why don't I want to run a million miles from this guy?

My throat throbs with sensation from where he pressed his fingertips into it, and between my legs, my pussy matches the beat.

I turn to face him. He looks into my eyes, his lips twisting into a wicked smirk as he sees the ambivalence in me.

"Oh, *I* see," he says. He grips my chin firmly and tilts my head back, making me look at him. "Let's fucking try that again, shall we? Are you a bad girl, Ali? Is that what you want to be?"

The words come out of my mouth before they're fully formed in my head.

"I want to be a good girl."

"Get on your knees and prove it."

Leo's hands fly to my head, pushing me to the ground. It doesn't occur to me to object. He undoes his zipper, freeing his cock, and I balk at the thought of fitting him inside me. I don't know if it's because he needs to come, or whether it's that big all the time, but his girth looks like a challenge.

He sees my eyes widen, and he laughs, gripping his cock at the base. His other hand grabs a fistful of my hair.

"It'll be okay, baby." He bounces the shiny tip on my chin. "I'll make it fit. But you better get it good and wet first."

He lets go of his cock, and I tip my head back as he feeds his erection into my mouth. He's warm and so hard, the veins straining his skin. I taste the salty dew at the tip and kneel up so I can take more of him.

Leo gives a low moan and reaches for his shirt, pulling it off over his head. I glance up and catch his eye.

Fuck. He's glorious. The v-shaped slice of his hipbones frames his cock, rising into flat, muscled abs and a broad chest.

To my delight, he's tattooed—a wolf on his pectoral muscle and a dagger with roses on the other side. The artwork is intricate; clearly, he can handle pain.

The shirt is gone, and he flexes his powerful arms above his head before suddenly pulling away from me and sitting on the edge of the bed.

"Come here," he says. "Get nearer to me. Right at my feet."

I shuffle forward. "Like this?"

"Good girl."

I feel a flare of arousal in my core. The way he says that... it messes with me. I don't know why I love it, but I do. The evidence is soaking through my dress.

Leo strokes the back of my neck with his fingertips as though he's working a knot loose. I sigh as the tension in my muscles eases off.

Then his hand wraps around my neck, gripping like a vice as the other takes hold of my hair once again.

"I'm gonna fuck your face until I've messed up your mascara and your throat is sore, *tigritsa*."

I have no chance to respond before he pulls my head toward him, impaling my mouth on his cock. I gasp and choke as the throbbing head smashes into my soft palate, drawing a wet, gagging sound from me.

"That's what I wanna fucking hear," he says, pumping his hips to meet me. "You want this?"

No. No. I want to say it, but I can't. Not just because his erection is pistoning in and out of my throat, preventing me from speaking, but also because it would be a dirty lie.

How does he know? How does he know what he's *doing* to me by treating me this way?

Leo's cock glistens, coated with thick saliva dragged up from deep in my throat. The impact makes my tonsils painful as he holds me in place, fucking my mouth. He growls when I lash my tongue at the sweet spot beneath the head of his cock.

My clit is tender and in desperate need of attention. Every time I shift, I feel it brushing my pussy lips, wet and sore with sensitivity. I reach between my legs.

Before I can touch myself, Leo stands, and I'm forced to my feet, held almost aloft by his hand around my neck. I moan as he grasps his cock, rubbing it between my legs.

"So wet." He laughs at my whimpers. "You want me to fuck you, Ali? You want me to wreck that tiny pink pussy?"

I can't nod. I can't speak. As he slides his cock along my slit, I fix my eyes on him.

Yes. Fuck me. I don't care who you are, and I don't care why you're like this or why this feels so incredible. Don't ask. Just take.

Leo sees what he wants to see. I don't know whether something in my eyes gives my thoughts away or my slippery sex is doing all the talking, but he reads me loud and clear.

"Birth control?" he asks.

"Pill. I'm clean."

"Likewise. I'm glad because fuck knows I wanna pump you full of my come."

He steps out of his pants and pushes me backward onto the bed. I pull my dress over my head, showing him my naked body. He towers over me, pumping his cock as he looks me up and down.

"Not a single angle to be seen," he murmurs. "You're all curves. Luscious, rounded curves."

My typical shyness is nowhere to be seen. Usually, I'd try to cover up a little or strike a flattering pose, but I don't care what I look like because I can see what I'm doing to him.

His attention is so absolute, so sincere. He looks at me like it's not enough to fuck me - he wants to *worship* me. I feel desired, and it's incredibly arousing. The sight of this chiseled sex god jerking off over me will get me through many a cold, lonely night in the future, but right now, I'm staying in the moment.

I lie back and open my legs wide as Leo looms over me. He's still holding his cock, lining it up with my entrance as he lowers his weight onto my body. The feel of his tip nudging my aching hole is more than I can stand.

Leo retakes hold of my neck. When he applies the pressure, the leftover sting of his earlier grip is relieved. He lowers his lips onto mine, kissing me passionately as he eases into my pussy.

I wince as he stretches me, groaning against his mouth, and he chuckles. The hand on my neck shifts enough for him to slip his index finger between my teeth.

"Fair's fair, *tigritsa*. Hurt me good. I know you want to."

His cock pushes inside, stretching my internal walls and lighting up all my nerves. Despite my wetness, I must relax and breathe steadily to take him. I clench my jaw, biting hard enough to make him hiss through his teeth.

"I love it," he whispers hotly in my ear. "You take me like a good little slut." He bumps his hips as he bottoms out in my pussy, sending shockwaves of sensation through my abdomen. "You're hurting me, biting down like that. Do you enjoy hurting me, Ali?"

I turn my head slightly and look him in the eye as he takes his finger from my mouth. I see the skin is broken, blood running down his knuckle and along the back of his hand.

Seeing what I did gives me such a nasty thrill, yet leaves me feeling peaceful deep inside, as though the intensity of it is...cleansing, somehow.

"You *do* like it." Leo returns his hand to my throat, leaning his weight onto me just enough to make me gasp. "Good. I love a girl who can give as good as she gets, but right now, you're gonna take *this*."

He moves his body, pulling free of my clinging pussy before plunging back in to the hilt. He's not taking it easy, not letting me get used to him. My tits bounce off his chest as he holds my legs apart with his free hand, opening me up and making more space for him to fuck me.

The stretching pain gives way to a molten, searing pleasure as he pounds me. I feel so full of him. He bites my nipples roughly, pinning me to the bed and pinching my throat harder.

I should hate how rough he is, but he's so fucking turned on by me, and it makes me feel like the hottest woman on Earth. He's lost in my soft skin and clutching pussy, unable to get a hold of himself, muttering filthy things in my ear.

"You fucking dirty bitch." Leo reaches down to slap my ass. "You want it like this? Do you like me railing you? 'Cause I'm gonna fucking ruin you, Ali."

With a grunt, he withdraws from me and rolls me, grabbing a fistful of my hair as he pulls me onto all fours. Before I can register what's happening, he slams into me from behind, nearly knocking me onto the floor. His other hand envelops my throat again, his palm warm on my sore skin.

"Touch your clit," he commands. "I'm gonna fuck you hard and deep, and when I start, I won't stop. Got it?"

"Yes," I manage, reaching for my pussy as I feel Leo slide out of me.

The man means what he says. I brace my hips and tense up against the onslaught as he ravages me, my pussy aflame with ecstasy. It doesn't take more than a minute before my climax smashes through me, and I cry out, grinding onto Leo's cock as my pussy spasms and gushes.

The feeling is enough to tip Leo over the edge too, and with a groan, he slams into me one last time and then comes deep inside me. He pulls out of my pussy and sits back on his heels as I try to move.

"No, stay there," he says.

I don't move, but I feel suddenly vulnerable. My ass is in the air, asshole and pussy on show, come running out of me.

"Leo, I—"

"Can come again," he says, finishing my sentence. "You gonna be a good girl and come again for me?"

He doesn't wait for an answer. I open my mouth to say that I need to rest, but his fingers on my slick pussy lips silence my protests.

"It's so hot seeing me drip out of you," he says.

I feel his fingertips moving over me, scooping up the come. He pushes it back inside my pussy with two fingers, making my pussy walls shudder involuntarily with the aftershocks of my orgasm.

I close my eyes and drop my head onto my arms as he continues to work me, scissoring his sticky fingers inside my twitching cunt.

"So your come doesn't weird you out?" I gasp.

"Does it fuck." Leo swipes his thumb over my clit, and I jump. "It doesn't bother me in the slightest, believe me. I'd eat it from your ass if you wanted me to."

I can't think straight when he's touching me like this.

The dirty things he says will haunt my dreams. I know it. He's so primal, uninhibited, so nastily sexual. It makes me feel depraved in the best possible way.

Leo finds a rhythm, pumping his fingers in and out of me. Without thinking, I reach for my clit, rubbing it in time with his movements.

"Do it, *tigritsa*. Don't wait for me to give you pleasure. Fucking *take* it for yourself."

My legs shudder as my second orgasm quakes in my core. It's not as sharp a pleasure as when he was inside me. More a drawn-out release of rapture, the sex equivalent of taking a long sip of expensive cocoa.

Leo's finally done with me, and I collapse onto my front. He untucks the duvet under my leg and drapes it over us.

"The bed is soaked," he laughs.

I mumble an apology, but I have nothing left. Leo wraps around me, warming my limbs as sleep overtakes me.

5

Leo

When I wake up, it's still early.

Not that any light gets in here, but I can tell morning is on the way. I learned years ago to feel the rhythms of time passing and not depend on the sun.

I hear breathing in the room and leap to my feet, reaching behind the books on the nightstand and grabbing my handgun. It takes a full ten seconds for my brain to drop out of night-stalker vigilance mode and realize that there's no intruder. It's just Ali, her nose making a faint whistling sound as she sleeps.

Fucking hell. This is the problem with always being alone. I don't know how to handle having another human being around who I'm not trying to kill.

Why didn't I kick her the fuck out?

The answer comes from the bit of my brain that I fucking hate, the bit that forgets to lie to me.

Because it's cold, she feels good, and you like her enough to sleep beside her.

All good reasons but none of them have ever been sufficient before.

It's not as though I'm celibate. Because I have no real identity, I can be whatever version of myself gets results.

If I want a woman, I can get one. Usually an uptown divorcée or bored businessman's daughter, not a pretty little sneak thief in patched-up Vera Wang.

I'm also bemused as to why I brought her here.

I lied when I said I don't like hotels. I love them, and all my expenses are covered in my line of work. This place is where I go when I want to be me and get my head out of the noise.

So why did I bring a woman here for the first time ever?

I watch Ali sleep. Her hair is no longer sleek and polished, her bangs curling on her forehead. Her full breasts are exposed to my gaze, her rosy nipples peaky in the slight chill. She smiles a little as though remembering a joke.

Her eye makeup is streaked across her cheeks.

Jesus. What the *fuck* did I do to her? What did she do to *me*?

I didn't mean to go all out like that.

My tendencies are the kind that only a brave or stupid psychotherapist would want to tackle. I don't care about boundaries or limits or any of the shit that a normal human being needs from a lover.

I don't like people *at all*. That's what makes me a great assassin. I'm isolated because I don't mix well with others.

On a psychological level, I understand that it's not okay. But I don't *care*.

My finger stings. I look at the raw little gouge where Ali's teeth pierced my skin. I allowed her to hurt me, and she didn't think twice.

I hope it leaves a scar. To be marked for life by that sexy bitch would be an honor. It'll be the most commitment I've ever given a woman, that's for sure.

My cell phone screen is too bright. I wince and turn the backlight down, checking messages.

Shit. I forgot to check in.

Ben is my handler, but Pavel gets the final confirmation of a job well done. I have several missed calls from both of them.

Pavel doesn't text often. He's an old man who thinks text messages are too easy for me to ignore. He has a point. His angry bellowing over voicemail is more impactful than a few typed-out expletives. I love the old bastard, but he does get worked up easily.

I'm not calling him back now, but the point is made.

This is fucking sloppy of me. I'm *working*. Just because I meet a woman who tempts the fucked-up parts of my psyche doesn't mean I can disregard the details.

I open the window shutter and look out onto the street. A purplish haze behind the building heralds the coming dawn.

On the street outside is a car that wasn't there when we arrived a few hours ago. As my eyes alight on the man in the driver's seat, he ducks out of sight, but I recognize him immediately. I close the shutter, leaving it open an inch.

Ah. We have a vigilante in our midst.

The security guard from the hotel. The guy I was ready to beat to a pulp for grabbing Ali. Either he's picked up a lead from somewhere and trailed us, or he works for some enemy of mine and thinks he's got the drop on me.

Typical. Another bolt-hole gone.

This house belonged to a filthy old cunt who had been procuring underage girls for some politician or other, but he got in a mess when he abducted and raped the daughter of one of the Gurin Bratva's longest-standing allies. He let her go when he realized his mistake, but it was too late by then, and I took a hefty extra fee to fuck him up before I killed him. No one asked any questions, and I've used his house as a base ever since.

I like to believe that particular execution balances out some others. I can't know for sure because the details of *why* I have to take someone out are of no interest to me. I don't care whether they deserve it, and as such, I cannot be bargained with. If it's my job to kill them, they're dead.

I glance at Ali. She isn't stirring.

I lean behind the desk and retrieve the black case containing my backup sniper rifle.

The shutter on this window creates a useful optical illusion; unless you're up close, it's impossible to tell that there's no glass in the window frame.

An inch of space. *Plenty.*

I screw the silencer onto the end of the rifle's barrel and load a single round into the chamber. I put my eye to the gap in the shutter.

The idiot in the car thinks his comedy duck-and-cover routine worked, and now he's sitting there, looking at his cell phone.

The rifle is weighty but perfectly balanced. I'm strong enough to fire it accurately without placing it on its stand, and I'm in a bad fucking mood anyway, so the challenge is welcome. I brace the weapon against my shoulder and line up the shot.

With a sharp but muted pop, the bullet pierces the parked car's windshield so neatly that the glass doesn't shatter. The man slumps over the steering wheel.

Ali screams.

I click on the safety and pull the gun back through the window, quickly putting it on the floor beneath the desk. When I look at Ali, she's sitting bolt upright, the duvet clutched to her chin. Her eyes are open, but they're glassy and unfocused.

"Papa," she whispers. "Help me."

I'm frozen to the spot. *What the fuck is going on?*

She's shaking. Subtly at first, but then it's like she's having a fit. I run to her, shaking her shoulders.

"Ali!"

She blinks hard before shoving me away.

"Get off me!" she shrieks. She jumps out of bed, taking the duvet with her.

I can't fuck around. I don't know what that guy's agenda was, and hopefully, he was just a fucking cowboy, but I have to get her out of here so I can bail. I shouldn't have let her stay in the first place.

"You need to leave," I say, pulling on my pants. "Get dressed and go. I'll give you a sweater and some cash for a cab."

She glares at me for a long moment.

"How *dare* you treat me like a whore?" she asks. "I need a shower, at least. Why are you being such a prick?"

Because I just shot a man dead right outside this building. I need to disappear. But I can't tell her that unless I'm gonna kill her too.

I throw a gray jersey at her. She catches it reflexively before throwing it on the floor.

"I am *not* gonna let you just—"

"Get. Dressed." My tone leaves no room for debate.

Ali puts on her dress and shoes, raking her fingers through her hair. My sweater swamps her frame, the sleeves covering her hands, and as she tucks her hair behind her ear, I'm hit with a sensation I don't fucking like.

She seems vulnerable all of a sudden. Not the rapacious minx I fucked all over the place only hours ago.

I turn away from her and dress, listening for the sound of sirens or other cars, but the street is silent. When I turn back to Ali, she's looking anywhere but at me.

"Look," I say, taking a step toward her. "I'll look you up when I'm next in town. Where do you live?"

"Fuck you." She's trying to sound harsh, but her voice has no bite. "I don't want to set eyes on you ever again. I have one of my episodes in front of you, and how do you respond? You make me feel cheap and throw me out."

Episodes? Is that what it was? What does that mean?

Despite everything, a clear desire cuts through me.

I want to stop time - stop the turning of the fucking *Earth*, even - so I can be with her until she feels safe again. I don't know who hurt her before today, but I want to see them suffer. Right now, though, it's me, and I can't take another moment of it.

I pick up my wallet and hand her a wad of bills. She snatches it and turns away, and before I can say anything else, she's gone, slamming the door behind her.

∽

I want to go after her, but I know it's a bad idea. My feet are moving anyway, but then my cell phone rings. I snatch it up from the desk and answer it.

"Fucking *what*?" I say.

Luckily for me, it's not Pavel but Ben.

"You didn't check in, for fuck's sake. Pavel is going nuts thinking his precious *Volk Smerti* is dead."

"You can see where I am, Ben. I didn't turn off my phone tracker either."

"Yeah, and do you think I'm gonna tell him you're at your hideout but didn't bother to check in? I assume you were fucking someone. *Tell* me you killed her."

No, Ben, I didn't. And this is the first time that even occurred to me. She was there at the scene of the hit. She could identify me.

She saw me naked. I don't let anyone see my identifying marks. Hell, I barely even *talk* to people.

"Yeah, no loose ends," I lie.

That's a real fucking whopper. Biggest load of bullshit I ever told Ben, and he's the nearest thing I have to a friend, so he's heard his share.

"I had to take out a security guard from the hotel," I say. I reach under the bed and pull out a jerry can. "Don't know if he followed me or what, but I think he was trying to be a hero. I gave him some shit back at the hotel, so it might just be that."

"I'll ask around. What's the plan now?"

I unscrew the cap on the can and pour gasoline onto the bed. It sloshes onto the rug, running off between the floorboards. I throw the laptop onto the mattress and add more gasoline, wrinkling my nose as the stench stings my nostrils.

"I'm coming home. Tell Pavel to calm the fuck down."

"I'll tell him, but it'll make no difference. He's super pissed at you."

"Job's done. I'll be back before it's light."

I hang up.

The stolen jacket is draped over the desk. I pick it up, looking for my car key. There aren't many places it could be, and I realize it's gone.

I go to the front door and open it. Of course, the car isn't on the drive.

Props to her.

There's no one on the street. Two minutes later, I have the dead security guard laid out on the bed. I throw the last of the fuel over him before heading out the door.

I leave with my phone, wallet, and the clothes on my back. In my pocket is the matchbook from the bar. I turn in the doorway and strike a match on the jamb, enjoying the pain as it burns too close to my finger.

I flick the match into the room. Flames lick along the gasoline trails, setting the bed alight, and I grin.

6

Leo

"So you murdered a man, got drunk, fell asleep, and then just didn't bother to call?"

Pavel is in a fucking shitty mood. Anyone would think I was married to him or something.

"Boss, I'm not gonna go over this again." I drain my drink and wave the empty glass at Kristen. "I got the job done. Brazier is as dead as you wanted, so I don't see the problem."

Kristen brings me more vodka in a fresh tumbler, and as I turn to take it, she sits on my knee.

If I were in a better frame of mind, I'd tease her a little. She wants a piece of me and doesn't care to hide the fact. Usually, I enjoy her attention, but today she's pissing me off. I shove her ass, pushing her back onto her feet.

"Don't," I scowl. "I'm busy."

She stalks out of the room, her face ugly with anger.

"Leo, you know the rules," Pavel says. "This was our hit - *my* hit - which means I'm in charge of it. If it came from outside, like an associate of ours, it'd be different. But you answer to *me*. Just remember, Leo - unless you get married and have a family, the *komissiya* will want *my* approval to accept you as my successor."

I sigh. Of course I know the rules, and this is the first time I've deviated from them. But I'll take his bitching in good humor.

Pavel is Pakhan. His wife couldn't get pregnant, and he refused to take a mistress. She died, and he has no known children, legitimate or otherwise. This is a problem or *would* be if it weren't for me.

He took me in when I was a kid after a rival of his killed my father, and he sent me to Moscow to train with the *Spetsnaz*, customary for enforcers since the early days of the Bratva. He's like a father to me, and in my turn, he'll ask the *komissiya* for permission to entrust his empire to my care.

"Okay, Pavel," I say, "I know you're pissed at me. Just let it go. No harm done."

"You're all I have, Leo." Pavel lights a cigar. "Everyone is afraid of you. If you slack off, it reflects on my leadership. On *me*. I know you want to be in charge, but you're not there yet."

"I know that." I sip my vodka. It's ice-cold and wonderfully sharp. "Don't worry about it. I'm *Volk Smerti*. No one can take that away from me."

Pavel isn't looking at me. His eyes rest on the portrait on the wall, as they always do when he's worried about something.

The picture is a studio photo taken many years ago. In the center stand Pavel's parents, flanked by their two sons. All of them are smiling, but no one looks comfortable.

"We were happy for a time, you know," Pavel says. He stands up and walks over the picture, his shoulders sagging as though his memories are weighing him down.

Pavel's half-brother Bogdan committed suicide nineteen years ago. I know this because the anniversary of the event just passed, and the old man gets this way every year. His mother took her own life too, so it's a sore subject.

"Boss, I didn't know Bogdan, but I'm sure he wouldn't have wanted you to wallow like this."

Pavel scoffs, stubbing out his cigar on the wall. "You *would* say that. Have you ever *felt* anything, Leo?"

Yes. But I don't want to think about that. About *her*. She crowds my mind until I can't think about anything else, and I need to keep her out.

"If I start feeling, I'd be less useful to you," I say.

Pavel looks at the picture for a long moment. He reaches out and touches his father's face.

"Love is sublime agony, my boy. You can be devoted to someone only for them to spit in your eye. My parents were lucky to have one another. To have a family."

I stay quiet.

I know little about family. My mother died when I was born, and my father was killed because he got mixed up in something. I never learned what - my father was a fucking *tailor*. He had no criminal connections. The worst thing he ever did was sew a lining crooked, but for some reason, he took up arms in a mob turf dispute and got shot for it.

"I'm gonna go find Ben," I say, setting my drink on the table. "Is he here? The girls seem to be avoiding me, and that's usually because that suave fucker is kicking around somewhere."

Pavel turns to face me, arching an eyebrow. "You're better looking than Ben, but the girls are afraid of you. That asshole has that sophisticated charm that the likes of you can't compete with."

I smile. He knows damn well that I've been through every girl working in this club, and none of them held my attention for an hour, never mind an entire night.

I flex my finger, my knuckle breaking the wound open yet again. A bead of crimson appears, and I thrill at the sight, remembering Ali biting down as she took my cock in her tight little cunt.

Don't think about her now, for fuck's sake.

Ben is downstairs at the bar, nursing Sambuca and flirting with one of the new dancers.

"Hi Leo," the girl purrs, looking over Ben's shoulder. He spins around on his stool, extending a hand to me.

"The man himself," he says as we shake. "Boss give you a hard time?"

"Nah." I pull a seat up beside him. "He's just that way out. Time of year."

Ben frowns, not understanding. Then the realization hits him.

"Oh, you mean Bogdan. Fucking hell. You'd think he'd be over it."

I wave a finger at the barkeep, and he brings me a glass. I pour out a shot of Sambuca.

"I think it's incredible how Pavel can keep Bogdan's memory sacred." I down the shot and grimace. Good vodka is a hard act to follow. "His brother took his own life and took his wife and kid with him. Fucking low thing to do."

"Particularly when his mother killed herself too. It's a lot for Pavel to cope with, that's for sure."

I notice the girl Ben was talking to, still loitering awkwardly at his side. Ben turns to her.

"Scooch, *krasivaya*," he says. "I'll call you."

She pouts for a moment before doing as she's told. Ben turns back to me.

"Nice piece of ass, don't you think?"

I nod non-committally. *Not really. Not anymore.* There are many beautiful girls here, but as far as I'm concerned, they could be mannequins.

"Ah, yes!" Ben says, slapping the bar. "I forgot. You got your freak on, didn't you? I can tell you got nasty because if you hadn't, you'd have told me all about her already."

I rub my bleeding knuckle with my thumb like it's a talisman.

I don't want to talk about her.

"You know how it is," I say. "Women have nothing to offer me except somewhere to put my cock. And God knows I have nothing to offer *them* once I've got what I wanted. I leave them sore, and maybe they want more, but the important thing is that I *leave.*"

"Whatever you say." Ben reaches inside his jacket and pulls out a thick wad of bills, handing it to me. "As punishment, you're only getting half. Don't start on me. Boss's decision."

I take the money and pocket it. There's a lot I could say, but I'll take it up with Pavel.

I stand and head for the door.

"Leo, I meant to ask," Ben says, "what happened to your car? I tracked it and found it burned out. You get compromised?"

I smile.

Quite the tantrum. I appreciate Ali's methods. Very theatrical.

"Yeah, I had to abandon it. Fuck knows what happened there."

Ben shrugs. "I guess some crackheads got hold of it. Still, no forensics, no trace, no problem. Right?"

"Right. Now I'm going home. Don't call me."

∿

I lie on my bed and look at the ceiling.

Something fundamental has shifted in my mind.

I don't know what I can do except stay the fuck away from her. Luckily, that should be easy, if only from a practical point of view.

I can't ask Ben to look her up because her connection to me puts her in danger, plus I didn't fucking kill her when I *knew* she could identify me. This is a far more significant breach of the rules than just not checking in with Pavel, and he's pissed off enough as it is.

I close my eyes and curl my hands into fists, cursing God for putting her in my path.

I can't find Ali. I wouldn't know where to start.

Thank fuck for that.

7

Three years later...

Ali

"Do you want chicken or beef?" Roxy asks.

"It doesn't matter. There's no actual meat in either. It's just MSG and placebo that makes it taste of anything."

"What's placebo?"

Roxy hands me an instant ramen pot and a fork.

I smile. Roxy is uneducated but not stupid. I trust her with my life and with things that are even more important than that.

"Did you get whatever the thing was?" Roxy slurps her noodles. "You know, for Mooky?"

"You mean the airborne gonorrhea that I'm certain he has? I think he's so riddled with STIs that he's patient zero of a new strain of evolved super-bugs."

"Urgh." Roxy wrinkles her nose. "Like Pokemon. But not."

I laugh. "But to answer your question, yes. It was a data stick. I stole it, gave it to him, and got paid. But I managed to pick something else up while I was there."

I reach into my purse and pull out a battered voice recorder.

"Now, I know it's got that pre-loved look," I say, holding it out to her, "but beggars like us can't be choosers. It works just fine. You should find it much easier to keep up in class now."

Roxy puts down her noodles and comes over to my seat, taking the voice recorder from me. She turns it in her hands, taking in the scratches and dings.

"It's perfect!" She flings her arms around me.

Roxy takes counselling classes whenever she can, trying to build up enough credits to get an on-the-job training post at the children's home. She's dyslexic and needs more help, but she doesn't want to piss off the tutor who will recommend students for the job. I try to help her because she's a wonderful person who is fantastic with children. She has a shot at helping the kids, something I wish I could do.

But I can't. Not with my criminal record.

"I'm glad you're happy," I say with a smile. "But there's not much money left from the job. This palace of shit where we reside is home for another six months, but it's gonna be ramen and cheap vino for Christmas dinner."

Roxy smiles. "That's alright, Ali. You can't do any more than you're doing now. And you got more for that one gig than you would for a thousand pocket dips."

She's not wrong.

I don't usually take risks like that, but I desperately needed the money. Besides, Mooky is alright. I wouldn't call him a friend, but he's sent a few decent jobs my way over the years and never ripped me off.

I didn't ask who wanted the USB stick or why, but it doesn't take a genius to figure it out. It's presumably storing information the owner doesn't want in the public eye. Details of bribes, blackmail-worthy hobbies, that kind of thing.

The less I know, the better. And with that risky escapade done and dusted, I can take a step back for a little while.

I hear rapid little thuds outside the door and sigh.

Luna has struggled to sleep since I put her in her big-girl bed, and it isn't quiet outside. The white noise machine only does so much to block out the sound of Christmas festivities in the streets below us.

The door opens, and my little girl is standing there beside my chair, rubbing her eye with her tiny fist. At just over two years old, she's bright and articulate, with a tendency to climb things. But she has nightmares, and she doesn't like the dark.

I don't blame her. I have nightmares too, and although I force myself to sleep without the light, I sometimes feel like the darkness is crawling over me.

"Mumma," Luna yawns. "Noisy."

"I know, baby." I pick up my cheap knock-off music player and connect the over-ear headphones to Bluetooth. "How about I put your music on for you? See if we can get you back off to snoozyland?"

She nods, taking my hand. She turns to throw Roxy a wave.

"G'night Woxy," she trills.

"Night night, angel face," Roxy replies. "Try to get some sleep now."

∼

Luna's hand is cold, and I feel the gnawing shame that hits me a hundred times a day.

I can't keep my apartment warm or even dry. A bucket in the corner of my child's bedroom catches drips from the leak in the roof.

Lena's room used to be mine, but after she was born, I gave it up to her. She was never a good co-sleeper - she was desperate to get away from me and into her own bed. I got hold of an old crib for her, but it was so splintered and wrecked that Roxy and I had to spend hours wrapping every inch in duct tape. I couldn't get a mattress, so we pulled the foam out of one of our couch cushions, and Roxy stitched a cover together by ripping apart a couple of pillowcases.

The time of year makes it worse. We don't even have a proper Christmas tree, just a tiny one groaning under the weight of the tinfoil baubles Luna and I made.

Luna doesn't know how poor we are. She doesn't understand how we live. Roxy helps me to look after her, and I'm grateful because she's the only person in the world I trust with my baby. But that means Roxy isn't bringing money in, so our shitty situation isn't going to improve any time soon.

I tuck my daughter into bed, pulling the coverlet up to her neck. She tugs at the headphones, and I put them on her.

"Here you go," I say, stroking her cheek as I find her songs. "You like this playlist." I adjust the volume and press play.

Luna loves David Bowie. So do I, but really, it's all Roxy's doing. She blasts his music whenever she gets the chance.

My child's eyes are already closing. Her little fingers stroke my bracelet, the one I never take off. As I tuck her hair behind her ear, she nudges my hand away from her face.

I smile. Only a secure and well-loved kid knows they can safely turn down affection. There's always more to be had.

My mother and father would have adored her.

Tears prick my eyes. With a quick kiss, I leave my little girl to rest, closing her door behind me.

∼

True to form, Roxy is watching Labyrinth.

"If you're not listening to Bowie, you're watching him," I say as I return to my seat and pick up my food. "Don't you find his package distracting in that leotard?"

Roxy grins. "I warned you about it before we first watched it."

"No, you didn't. Your exact words were, 'David has a large part in this movie.'"

Roxy sniggers as she pours us some wine. "Not my fault you misunderstood!"

We lapse into silence.

I'm not watching the movie. My eyes rest on the photo in a frame on the small table beside me.

It's a picture of Luna and me. She's wearing a purple beanie, grinning like the cheeky monkey she is. I'm trying to hold the phone still to get a good selfie, but laughing as I fuck it up. The picture is wonky and slightly blurred, but it's still my favorite.

My daughter's beautiful ocean eyes.

It's hard to see Leo every time I look at her.

We had one night together, but it was enough to change everything. My entire life is divided into BL and AL - Before Leo and After Leo.

I don't know why my contraceptive pill let me down. I don't know why I didn't get an abortion either, but the thought never entered my head. As soon as that little test strip turned blue, I knew I would be a Mommy. That was the focus of my life from that day forward. Everything I've done, every risk I've taken, and every crime I've committed since were to keep a roof over our heads and put food on our table.

Should I have brought a kid into my shambolic life? Probably not. But I don't regret it. Luna is the reason that I keep striving, and it's for her I dream the impossible.

A clean slate. If I could get my record expunged, I could get a regular job and live an everyday life. I refuse to let go of hope.

But I've given up on *him*.

I told Leo I never wanted to see him again, but somehow I still thought he'd come back for me. Stupid, I know. But he reached into my soul and brought something to life that night. He made me feel so raw, so real.

I'm a complete nobody. No home, no family, no future.

Leo looked at me like I was the lock and he was the key. I'd give anything to feel that intensity again, even for a moment.

I've been thinking about him for too long. Whenever I lose myself in memories of Leo, my tough shell cracks, and I feel too much.

Don't cry, Ali. Don't let Roxy see...

Too late. Roxy is at my side, taking the wine glass from my hand. I didn't notice I was spilling it on myself.

"C'mon, babe. You take the bed tonight. You need it."

"No," I insist, wiping my cheeks with my sleeve. "You need to sleep properly because you have Luna all day tomorrow. I'm fine in my usual spot on the couch."

Roxy frowns at me, but she knows better than to argue.

"If you're sure. I'll check on the munchkin and turn off her music for her."

"Okay. Night."

Roxy leaves the room, turning off the television as she goes. I can hear 'Jingle Bell Rock' being played outside somewhere, but it's not loud. The streets are getting quieter as the bars close.

I stand up and rummage through the drawer, looking for what I need.

I should have gotten rid of Leo's sweater, but I couldn't. It still carries a faint trace of his scent, and when I need comfort, it's the only thing that helps. As I pull it over my body, I tuck my nose into the neckline, breathing him in.

I drag the fur throw from the back of the armchair and tip the recliner. It doesn't go flat and makes a weird noise when I shift around, but I'm used to it.

The tears dry on my face as I lie in the dark, watching each set of passing car headlights chasing the shadows on the cracked ceiling.

∼

Leo

It's four in the morning, and I'm sitting on the roof.

This is usual for me. I don't sleep anymore. Insomnia and I met about three years ago, and the bastard moved in with me.

I tried to evict him. He won't leave. So we hang out together until he deigns to fuck off and let me crash for a couple of hours.

My subconscious is a sneaky bastard. It hides my true thoughts and intentions from me most of the time, but now and again, it throws me a curve ball. I guess it doesn't like me very much.

So recently, in the small snatches of sleep I get, I've been dreaming of Ali.

Not the dreams I've been having for years, though. Not the ones where I'm at her side, dominating her thoughts, her body, and her life. I love those fucking dreams, and if it weren't for those, I wouldn't care if I never slept again.

But recently, it's been getting sinister. I look for her in my sleep, but I can't find her every time. I wake up sweating, my chest tight.

I got very fucking close to asking Ben for help to find her. But he and I aren't as tight as we were. He's been complaining about his place in our organization, saying he wants assurances he'll move up when I'm running things. Assurances he could have gotten easily before he started getting pushy.

Pavel is old. He doesn't care as he should. Acts like Ben is some bolshy kid who'll grow out of it, but the guy is thirty-five years old. I'd have heard about it if I'd thrown my weight around like that when I was his age.

Things are too calm these days.

Gone are the days when I had more jobs than I knew what to do with. It was fun because you might be in a queue if you were expecting a visit from me. Plenty of time to get very scared and make ludicrous bargains in an effort to avoid what's coming to you.

Not that it makes any difference to the outcome. No one ever calls me off.

I still have a one hundred percent success rate. If *Volk Smerti* is coming to kill you, it is happening.

My reputation is the only thing keeping Pavel on his throne. I could remove him if I didn't love the old cunt, but that's unnecessary. Whatever Ben thinks, he's not in the running.

It's all mine to take, and I'm happy to wait.

I climb into the open skylight and down the ladder into my loft. The moon is directly above, framed in the window, and I lie on the floor, looking up at it.

Ali sleeps somewhere under the same moon, watched by the same stars. I wonder whether she thinks about me as much as I think about her, but I seriously doubt it.

I came back from the hit on Judge Brazier a different man.

All my experiences in life made me who I am. I look inside, and there's nothing to see. Pavel says it's better that way - he loved people and lost every one of them. All his power never made up for that.

No woman ever made me want to feel anything—quite the opposite. A couple of girls have professed their love for me, and many more have tried to get close, but I'm all too aware that there has to be a real, human connection along the way.

I'm not capable of that. And if I'm honest with myself, that's a lot of the reason I never tried to find Ali.

I flex my finger, feeling the familiar sting.

The tiny wound Ali gave me never quite healed because I won't let it.

I'd say I don't want to hurt her, but that's not true. I *do* want to hurt her, but it's more than that.

I want her to hurt me right back. She drew out something feral in me, and I want to feel it again.

~

Ben sits in the sunroom, drinking coffee.

"It's seven-thirty. Why the fuck are you here so early?"

"Good morning to you, too," I say, pouring a cup for myself from the French press. "You said there's a job for me. What's the news?"

Pavel lives here with his housekeeper, Zoya. She's been around for years, keeping both his house and his secrets. But since Ben took a post as his personal bodyguard, he's here day and night. Pavel never mentioned it to me until they'd already agreed on it between them.

"It's nothing exciting." Ben is flicking through a file of papers. "Just a routine hit."

I reach for the file, but Ben snatches it away and smiles.

"Don't you want to hear the juicy details?"

"I can read."

Ben rolls his eyes. "If you did less rooftop brooding and more sleeping, you'd be less of a cranky bastard. I'm fucking with you, anyway. There's nothing to tell. It's an outside job."

I raise an eyebrow. "Really? It's been a while since the *komissiya* approved one. So we don't know who the client is?"

"Nope. They know, but we're in no position to find out. They came to me to give you the job because Pavel has nothing to do with it, but he knows you've been called up."

Oh great. Is Ben giving orders now?

"So why all the secrecy?" I ask. "I have to assume it's not Bratva business in the first place."

"If it were, we'd have been told. We knew all about it when you took the Judge out, and remember that fuckwit police commissioner? You fucked his wife the same night you shot him!"

I laugh, but inside I'm wincing. Yeah, I remember.

That was before Ali. Now I keep my business as clean as I can. Just do my job and go home.

Ben taps the file. "What little we have is in the dossier," he says. "Open and closed case, it seems. As usual, it's a forty-eight-hour exclusivity clause. If you don't take out the mark by then, the client can do what they like, but you're dead. Even Pavel won't be able to do anything about it."

I smile. Ben loves giving me this little speech, but he knows damn well it'll be a cold day in hell before that happens.

Ben hands me the file. I knock back the coffee and turn to leave.

"Oh, one more thing, *Volk Smerti*."

I turn back to face him. His mocking tone has got my back up.

"What?"

"Don't fall in love. She's a smokeshow."

I wait until I'm back in my car before looking at the dossier. The nausea I'm feeling is probably down to the coffee, but I can't shake the sense that something is wrong.

I sit in the driver's seat and draw a deep breath, opening the cardboard cover.

I was almost expecting it because it's the best and worst thing that could happen. But it's still a shock to see her.

Ali.

A grainy still from a security camera and a couple of smaller snaps taken with a long lens. The photos aren't good quality, but it's her.

I should know. I see her face every night in my dreams.

Her hair is longer, but it's still the same raven color, with the same straight bangs. She doesn't look any older, but she does look a little beat down. In one photo, she's wearing an oversized Parka and skinny jeans, and I can see she's slightly too thin for her frame, her collarbone sharper than I remember.

This woman has caused me pain every day for three years. It's taken every scrap of my self-control not to throw caution to the wind and track her down so I can lie at her fucking feet and worship her. She's been killing me just by living her life without me.

And now I have to kill her.

8

Ali

"Are you alright, dear?" the old lady asks.

She's patting my arm, and I know I need to look at her, answer her, say *something*, but I can't. My groceries are all over the floor where I dropped them, cheap dented tin cans rolling away. The store assistant is picking them up and re-packing the bag.

Twenty seconds ago, I was doing okay.

I managed to get enough crappy canned food to last Roxy and me a week, and I kept it under ten dollars, so that meant I could go to the drugstore and fill Luna's prescription. I'm supposed to get her the long-acting bronchodilator, but it's too expensive, so I get the short-acting one. I know the dampness in my apartment aggravates her asthma, but there's nothing I can do about that. Still, I was getting by.

Then I saw Leo.

I mean, it *can't* have been him. But the man who walked out of the 7-Eleven opposite stopped me in my tracks.

I saw him as he pushed the door and stepped onto the street. His hair tumbled from his scalp, the same sandy blonde, and he raked his fingers through it as he stopped to look at his cell phone.

It was when he looked at *me* that I dropped my shopping.

He had my daughter's eyes. They locked on mine for a split second, and I felt like my soul had been seared with a red-hot poker.

A truck drove by and stopped at the lights, obscuring my view for a few seconds. When it moved, he was gone.

Now I'm standing here, blinking rapidly, trying to make him reappear. Because if I'm going insane, I'll go quietly to my madness with a smile. As long as I can see him again.

∼

"You got ravioli?" Roxy says, rummaging in the bag. "Awesome! Save some for me, won't you?"

"Sure."

Roxy shoots me a look. "There's something wrong with you. You've *never* agreed to save ravioli for me. You're territorial about it."

She's right. The truth is, I have no intention of eating it. Ever since I had my hallucination, I've been feeling sick to my stomach.

"Did you have...you know." Roxy glances at Luna, but she's playing with her blocks and not listening to us. Roxy lowers her voice anyway. "One of your attacks?"

"I don't know. Kind of?" I twist my fingers together as I speak. "I'm just tired. I'm glad of a night off tonight. But don't get greedy, okay? It's kind of you to take my shift, but don't dip any pockets. You're not good enough at it, babe. Do your job, get paid for the night, and come home. Deal?"

Roxy and I pick up the odd waitressing gig. It's cash on the night, and no resumé is required, but it's very short notice. I can't face it tonight, but Roxy knows we need the money.

"Deal." Roxy throws Luna a Twinkie, and she squeals with joy. "I'm going now, so enjoy yourselves!"

"Bye bye Woxy!" Luna yells as the door closes behind her. I scoop my daughter onto my lap and grab the TV remote.

"C'mon, baby, let's decide. Fishy Gets Lost, or Monster Man and the Teapot?"

"Teapot!"

Beauty and the Beast it is. I tap a button or two, and the movie starts. Luna settles, warm in my arms, and I relax.

I have my baby girl, and that's all that matters.

∽

Leo

"Pavel, I want the information this time."

The old man either isn't willing to tell me, or he genuinely doesn't know. As much as I want to believe he's just stalling, I suspect it's the latter. He's far more interested in his dead brother's memorial floral display. Ten grand he's spending on flowers that will soon be as dry and decayed as his brother is.

"Do you think lilies are too morbid?" he asks. "Bogdan's wife Starla always loved them."

I don't give a fuck about dead Bogdan or murdered-by-her-own-husband Starla. But it would be a bad idea to say so.

"I don't know anything about flowers."

Pavel looks at me and frowns. "No, you don't. I don't know why I fucking asked you. What's the problem, Leo? You're giving me a headache."

Gotta tread carefully here. It's weird enough that I came back to the house after leaving with the dossier. Pavel's guards ignored me, but Zoya raised an eyebrow. It's stranger still that I sought Pavel out when he has nothing to do with this. But there's something about Ben's attitude that I'm not happy about, so I'm side-stepping the fucker and going straight to the Boss with my innocent questions.

"Just seems a shame, that's all," I say. "She's a pretty girl, lives in some downtown shit-hole. How much trouble can she be in?"

Pavel's expression is one I've seen before, but it's never been directed at me. It's the one he uses when his patience is about to snap.

"Leo, this is the first time you've ever shown even a passing interest in a mark. You like the look of her? Then go ahead and fuck her blind for all I care. But she needs to be cold before the sunrise after next. The *komissiya* have given their assurances to the client; as you know, they supersede me. I'm not telling you anything because I have *nothing* to fucking tell you."

This is more explanation than anyone else would get. I take in the tired, exasperated look on Pavel's face, and I see that I'm getting to him.

"Bad times, huh, Boss?"

Pavel nods. He slumps in his chair, and I'm struck by how much older he suddenly seems.

"I'm sick of this life, Leo. It's hard." He waves at me to sit, and I pull up a chair opposite him. "I did what I had to do to secure my future here, but the human cost has been great."

"Your brother. Yeah, I know."

"I don't know what happened. He and I didn't always get along, and he took himself away from the family after getting married, but I never knew why. I always meant to find a way to reconnect with him, but he didn't want this life of ours. Then he was gone, and it was too late."

I don't know what to do with my face. I'm going for somber attentiveness, but I probably look like I've had a lobotomy.

"Don't let things pass you by, Leo," Pavel says. He sighs deeply and closes his eyes. "I left it too long to do what needed to be done, and now I'm paying the price. Lucky I have you, right?"

"Sure thing, Boss."

I stand and stretch. Pavel wakes up from his malaise and seems embarrassed, like he's said too much.

"Go and do the job, Leo. When you return, we'll discuss handing you the reins. I'm an old man and I would prefer to act like one."

Four hours later...

I'm *so* fucking drunk.

I can't remember the last time I was this toasted. I'm not the type to lose control, but being inebriated is still a potential shortcut to making a foolish mistake.

The building beside Ali's block is a massage parlor, with a couple of shitty apartments above it. I paid way over the odds for the place. The elderly Thai lady running the joint took one look at me and knew I'd happily hand over plenty of greenbacks if it meant she wouldn't ask me any questions. She's clearly something of a mercenary, but it takes one to know one.

So now I'm shaking out the dregs of this bottle of vodka and wondering whether I'm gonna do it. I'm drinking because I need an excuse for whatever happens next.

My sniper rifle has been set up on its tripod stand for hours now. I've established a simple pattern.

Sit in the dark for a while. Stand up, look through the telescopic sight. See nothing but the back of Ali's couch and light from the TV. Feel a wave of relief that I can't see Ali because if I can't see her, I can't shoot her. Pour more vodka, knock it back, wait a while, and repeat.

I fucked up this afternoon.

My only thought was to case the neighborhood near her apartment and see what was nearby. Standard procedure. Nothing unusual.

But then I fucking *saw* her.

Clear as day, as beautiful as the first time. Our eyes locked across the busy street, and she dropped her groceries. I almost stepped into the traffic to get to her, but a truck blocked my way, and I got a hold of myself and bailed.

Serendipity is a bitch.

Fuck me. I want to see her again. I want to see the woman who moved her body against mine like she was made for me. The woman who ruined me entirely while letting me believe I was in charge.

Thoughts float around my addled mind.

What am I gonna do? I can't kill her. I have to kill her. She has no hope of getting out of this. Better I do it than someone else...

A flicker of movement catches my eye, and I'm on the gun, my finger nudging the trigger already as I focus on my target.

A woman stands up from the couch. The light from the television silhouettes her, but from the way she moves, I know it's Ali.

Someone else is in the room. A figure shifts the darkness as she moves through the frame as if she's walking across a cinema screen.

Ali's boyfriend?

Jealousy punches me in the gut. Then I remember that she lives with a female housemate, as per Ben's information.

Could the dossier be incorrect? It was hastily pulled together, and the information is minimal. All I needed to know was who and where, so it's possible that critical details were missed...

I shift the rifle, aiming my sight at the taller silhouette.

I don't give a fuck what the rules are or who that asshole is. If he lays a finger on her, I'll...

His hands reach out for Ali, and it's too late. Both figures drop out of sight as he claps a hand over her mouth.

I'm out the door and down the stairs in seconds, running into the street and over the road. The entrance to Ali's block hangs ajar.

Someone got here first.

When did they sneak in? I didn't see it happen. It's supposed to be an exclusive contract. I didn't expect anyone else to try and cut in front of me.

The elevator is out of order and looks like it was last operational during the Cold War. The graffiti on the door says, 'You're only ever going down.'

I slap open the door to the stairwell, pistol in hand. I'm at the bottom of the third flight when I see them.

In less than a second, I take in the whole scene.

The man has Ali by the neck. The sight of that alone makes me want to bleed him dry. His gun is pressed to her temple, and he's kicking at the backs of her knees, forcing her to move in front of him. Her face is streaked with tears, but she's fighting at the same time, her hands clawing at his. Her eyes blaze with fury.

He's so focused on her that he hasn't seen me yet, but a gasp of shock from Ali makes him look ahead and down the stairs.

Everyone freezes.

He whips the gun around to me, but I get off a shot first, piercing a neat hole in his balaclava. He falls over backward, taking Ali with him. She hits the ground hard and cries out in shock.

I have to get her out of here. Fuck knows who else is coming, and I'm caught way off guard.

I dash up the stairs to Ali. She's screaming as blood pools under the dead man's head.

I flip up the man's balaclava and frown. *I know this prick. What the fuck is he doing here?*

"You fucking shot him!" Ali cries.

"You'd prefer it if we'd tried to talk it out?"

I grab her arm and pull her to her feet.

Ali looks at me like she wants to kill me herself. Her expression is between terror and rage.

"Why are you here?" she yells. She drops her face into her hands. When she speaks again, her voice cracks. "You've come back to kill me, haven't you?"

The pain in her words burns me. I want to hold her, but part of me wants to fucking shake her.

She's no idea what will happen to *me* if I *refuse* to kill her.

"Come on." I pick up the dead man's gun and turn back down the stairs.

Ali doesn't follow me. Instead, she turns on her heel and goes back up the stairs.

"Ali!" I shout. She doesn't respond, but I hear her footsteps quicken.

I run after her, cursing to myself. She nearly gets murdered in her own apartment, I save her, and she fucking *runs away*? This is why I usually kill people and don't get involved.

I hear a baby crying somewhere. I hope the other residents don't decide to come and check out the action. Witnesses are a massive issue for me, so I prefer to be at the end of my rifle sight and not in anyone's face. I didn't even think about what to do when I saw the guy grab Ali; I could have just left him to it and solved all my problems that way.

I reach the corridor just in time to see Ali heading into her apartment. I'm only a few seconds behind her.

"Ali!" I say as I enter the apartment. "This is not a debate. You're coming with me if I have to carry you over my—"

Ali walks out of the bedroom.

She's carrying a child.

A little girl, still young enough to have a pacifier. The baby has headphones on, her cheeks wet with tears.

She turns her face to me and frowns, clinging to Ali's shirt.

I'm looking into curious turquoise eyes.

My eyes.

~

Ali

I never thought this moment would come.

My child's father is standing before me, a gun in his hand. I never believed for a second that he would come back to me, let alone like this.

"Don't hurt us, Leo," I whisper.

There's a long, painful silence. The air is heavy with unspoken regret.

He didn't know.

I don't know what's happening or why he's here. But whatever the reason, Leo didn't know about our baby. His face gives it away. He looks from her to me as though he expects us to vanish any second.

"What does she need?" he asks.

I want to tell him to go. To leave and never come back. There's no way it's a coincidence that he turned up on the same day that a masked man attacked me in my home.

But no one ever looked at me that way before. His eyes bore into mine, melting my resistance.

"I know what you're thinking, Ali. But what choice do you have? You'll die without me. Both of you."

"Okay," I say. "Her *name* is Luna. She needs her toy rabbit, inhaler, blankie, clothes…"

Leo clicks on the safety and puts his gun in the holster at his hip. I watch his hands as they move, remembering how they felt when he touched me that night.

He has a Band-Aid on his knuckle.

"Pack a few things for the two of you," he says. "I have a room over there." He points out of the window. "It's safer than here."

"My housemate will come home. I need to make sure she's safe."

"Mumma," Luna says sleepily. She drops her head onto my shoulder.

"I can deal with that," Leo says. "But we have to get out of here right now, Ali. Do you understand?"

"Yes."

Luna is almost asleep again. Leo cocks his head and looks at her.

"I can hold onto her while you get your stuff together." He holds out his hands.

I hesitate. The man has a fucking gun under his jacket.

Yeah. And he shot the guy who tried to abduct me a minute ago. I'd be dead if he didn't show up when he did. Luna too.

I pass my sleeping child to Leo. He leans her against his broad chest, supporting her with his arms. She opens her eyes for a moment, but then they close again.

9

Ali

I'm sure I'm going to wake up any second.

My child is sleeping peacefully on my lap as I sit in the dark. The slats in the window blind are slightly tilted, throwing stripes of cold light over the room. Leo hasn't spoken or looked at me in over an hour.

When we got to the room, I saw the rifle set up and knew the truth.

I was right - he came to kill me. He was ready to do it.

The empty vodka bottle gave me pause. If he's drunk, he's not showing it. He sits behind his rifle, looking at my apartment through the sight.

If I speak, will I break the spell? Will he disappear, only for me to wake up in a psych ward, lost in madness?

Bring it on. I don't care.

"Leo, I'm scared."

He doesn't turn around. Since he handed Luna back to me and took up his vigil, he has been as still as a statue.

"Leo," I say again, a little louder. "Answer me."

He doesn't look at me. When he speaks, his voice is drenched in anger.

"How the fuck could you put yourself in this position, Ali? You have a child. *My* child."

"What the hell are you talking about? I don't know what's going on here. I don't know who that guy was," my voice rises, "and what right do you have to give me shit when you have a gun pointing at my window?"

"Shut the fuck up." Leo whips his head around to glare at me. He speaks in a low, even tone, but the look on his face is enough to silence me.

I worked so hard to get past this.

I was forgetting him, or at least I could tell myself that. Now he's back.

Am I afraid of him? *Fuck yes.* I know nothing about him; reality has already bludgeoned my fantasy image of him to death.

But other feelings are crashing through me, too, however much I wish they weren't.

My phone buzzes beside me. It's Roxy, finally replying to my message.

. . .

The Regent? Why?

Because I need you to be someplace safe, someone tried to hurt me. Just go there and give your name. You have a room already. See you soon.

Okay.

"Was that your housemate?" Leo asks. "Is she going to the hotel?"

"Yes."

"Then so are we. My car is round the back." He shoots me a glance and, for the first time, a smile. "I had to get a new one about three years ago. But I guess you knew that."

∼

The concierge at The Regent is the definition of discreet. He swipes Leo's credit card without a word.

The room is actually a suite, a penthouse on its own private floor. When Luna sees Roxy, she wiggles away from me and toddles toward her outstretched arms.

"Woxeeee!"

Roxy scoops Luna up and hugs her tight. She looks at me, then at Leo.

"Holy shit," she says. "You're the man, aren't you?"

Leo raises an eyebrow. "Damn right, I'm the man."

I catch Roxy flushing a little. I can't blame her, but a possessive flare heats me inside, even though she's my best friend.

What the fuck is wrong with me?

If Leo sees it, he doesn't comment. He dumps my bags on the floor.

"Which of these belongs to you?" he asks. I point at the gray holdall, and he picks it up, leaving Luna's pink suitcase. She runs over and unzips it.

"Bunny?" she asks. I reach into the case and hand the toy rabbit to her, smiling as she wanders back to Roxy.

"Say goodbye, Ali," Leo says, nodding at our daughter.

Roxy looks up from playing with Luna.

"What do you mean, goodbye?" I ask. "I'm not going anywhere. You said you would bring us here to keep us safe while you work out what's going on!"

"I said whatever I had to say to get you to agree to bring Luna here. She'll be safe with Roxy. No one is looking for either of them *yet*, but you're a target. The last thing I need is collateral damage."

The way he says it makes me want to claw his eyes out.

"I'm not leaving my child, Leo!"

He snatches my wrist, yanking it to him, and my body bumps into his. His face is inches from mine.

"Get your head around this, Ali," he says. "I was hired to kill you, but I'm not going to do it. That means that I have to find out who wants you dead and why. And even if I *can* do that, the chances of us both surviving this are extremely remote. If you keep Luna with you," he grabs my chin with his other hand and looks me in the eye, "she *will* die."

Tears stream down my cheeks.

"This is *your* fault," I hiss. "*You've* brought this upon us."

Leo draws a deep breath. It's as though he's holding something back. Then he lets go of me.

Luna is staring at us. I wipe my face with my hand and plaster a big grin across my face.

"Gotta go now, baby!" I say brightly, squatting down to her height. "You stay with Roxy and go to bed. I'll see you soon, okay?"

I look over my shoulder at Leo. His expression is impossible to read.

I silently mouth the words I want to scream.

I hate you for this.

"There's a room for her," he says. "It should be set up." He looks at Roxy. "You'll stay here with Luna. Don't go out. Ring the desk if you need anything; they have my card on account."

Roxy is on her feet. "You can't just —"

"Please." I pick up Luna and cuddle her, feeling her warm little body against me. "Please, Roxy. What else can I do?"

Roxy says nothing more. I hand Luna to her, trying not to freak her out by clinging on as she leaves my arms.

"Bye, Mumma!" she says, flapping her hand at me. "Love you!"

"I love you too, baby."

Leo is already leaving, my holdall on his back. I follow him, stealing a last look at my child as I close the door behind me.

My heart is breaking. But what choice do I have?

∽

Leo

"I need answers, Ali."

The car is not the ideal place to have a meaningful conversation, but I need information, and I need it fast. I'm glad we're parked, though. There's no one around at this early hour except the occasional jogger.

Ali sits beside me in the passenger seat, her mouth set in a furious line. She hasn't spoken since we left The Regent, and I know she probably wants to kill me, but I don't give a shit.

"*You* need answers?" She turns in her seat, her gray eyes darkening with fury. I note the redness there too. She's been trying to fight back tears all the way here, and mostly she succeeded, but I see the shine on her cheek. "I think you need to tell *me* a few things first, don't you? You dragged me away from my daughter, and now I'm in the ridiculous situation where staying with you - the man who was going to *kill* me until he changed his mind - is the *safest fucking option*?"

I can't help but smile. That's the Ali I went crazy for. She's had a hell of a night, but despite zero sleep and a fuck of a lot of danger, she's screaming at me.

"What do you want to know?" I ask.

"Who the fuck *are* you?" She points at my face, her finger almost touching my nose. "Why did you want to kill me?"

I raise my eyebrows at her. "Get your finger out of my face, Ali. Now."

She does as she's told, but her stare doesn't waver.

"I work for Pavel Gurin. Do you know who that is?"

She nods.

"Killing you was just a task. I'm Bratva. It's not as though anything we do is pleasant."

I realize that something has changed. A lightbulb has come on in Ali's head, and she's looking at me with wide, fearful eyes. When she speaks, she suddenly sounds like a child.

"So you kill people?"

I think about lying but decide against it. If I want to get us through this, I need her to tell me the truth, so I can't start by bullshitting her.

"Ali, I kill people *all* the time." I give a slight shrug. " I can't be swayed or bribed or negotiated with. I'm the guy who comes in when it's gone beyond all that, and someone has to die."

She leans away from me, holding out her hand as though she's trying to ward me off.

"I knew it," she whispers. "You're *Volk Smerti*."

The door opens, and she's gone, pelting down the road barefoot. I don't know when she slipped off her shoes. I leap out of the car and go after her as she peels away into the park.

Fuck, she's so sly. Fast too, but she's struggling to keep up the pace. As I reach her, she collapses, rolling off the path and down a short grass verge.

I dive to the ground and grab her arms, leaning my weight over her so she can't wriggle free. Then I see her face.

Her breath comes in small, choked gasps like she's suffocating. I shift my body, so I'm not putting pressure on her lungs, but it's not making any difference. Her eyes are glassy, and she can't keep them focused on mine.

I pull her to her feet and grip her shoulders to keep her upright.

"Ali!" I say, shaking her. She manages to focus on my face. "Look at me. Keep looking at me."

I grab her chin to stop her from flailing her head around. Her knees give out, and she falls forward, but I catch her, holding her waist to keep her upright.

Her breath is stabilizing. A whimper escapes her throat, and I cradle her head in my hand, supporting her against my chest.

"Breathe, *tigritsa*."

Ali's hands pull at my shirt as though she's trying to claw her way under my skin and hide. From what, I don't know.

She looks up at me, and I don't stop myself.

I lower my lips to hers.

A bruising, crushing kiss. I've dreamed of the kiss for years, the only one I ever wanted. Ali stills, her arms wrapping around my neck as her tongue delves into my mouth.

Abruptly, she shoves me away.

"Jesus fucking Christ!" she cries. "What is *wrong* with you? I panicked, and you took advantage of me. I didn't mean for that to happen."

"What the fuck *did* happen?" I ask. "I thought you were gonna die on me right here."

"Would have solved all your problems, wouldn't it?" she snarls.

We stare at one another. A potent mix of emotions color the moment - rage, fear, desire.

I want her fire to burn me.

I want her to *hurt* me.

But most of all, I want to fuck her until her fury is spent and she's a quivering, wrung-out mess.

10

Ali

We're holed up in a studio loft twenty minutes south of my neighborhood. We returned to the other place long enough for Leo to retrieve his stuff. He loitered in the stairwell of my building while I collected some important things of my own.

I came out to find Leo raiding the pockets of the dead guy, whose stiffening corpse was still lying in a heap on the landing. I looked on in disgust as Leo pocketed the man's wallet before dragging the body down the stairs, bagging it up, and putting it in the dumpster.

"Someone will find that," I said.

"Yep, but I will get one of our people to give local law enforcement a heads-up, so they don't make a fuss. Besides, they'll be glad to see the back of him."

I asked no more questions, and after Leo made a brief phone call, we came here.

On the way, Leo explained a few things to me about how his world works. He works for his Pakhan, Pavel Gurin, who leads his particular branch of the Bratva. The *komissiya* - a commission of Bratva leaders who oversee the activities of all the factions and impose rules and sanctions - took a job from someone who wants me dead. As per usual, they sent Leo to do the job. So far, so blah in the fucked-up world of the Russian mob.

And Leo Zhubarev, the father of my child, is *Volk Smerti*.

Not just a Bratva man. Not even just a murderer. He's a professional assassin who kills without conscience or morals. The only rules he has are the ones imposed by others - inside him, there are no principles to be found.

So why am I still alive?

"Let me get this straight," I say. "You turned up, got tooled up to fucking *kill* me, then someone else got to me first, and you rescued me instead?"

Leo is in the kitchenette, pouring drinks. He's shirtless, a fact I'm doing my best to ignore. But I can't deny he's fucking beautiful in his sweatpants, hair damp from his shower.

"Yep, that's it." He sits on the couch beside me, handing me the whiskey. I take a sip, the alcohol searing my tongue.

"And this place? Don't tell me. This is the dead guy's apartment, isn't it?"

"Kind of." Leo crosses his ankle over his knee and leans back. "He was a bounty hunter. He doesn't work for anyone, so he keeps all his pay but doesn't have anyone looking out for him. No one will give a fuck that he's dead. I got it checked out, and it turns out this is his long-term lease under a false name. So we might be able to stick around and stop running."

His knives and guns are laid out casually on the tabletop as though it's perfectly normal. He swills the drink in his hand. "This is good stuff. Just like old times." He knocks the whiskey back in one and turns to me.

"You and I will die, Ali, unless you get your head in the game. Stop asking *me* questions and start asking them of *yourself*. Who might want to kill you?"

"I take the occasional theft-to-order gig for the money. I stole a USB data stick about a month ago, but that's all I can think of."

"That's more like it. Tell me about this data stick."

I furrow my brow. "They stored it at a downtown office in a safe. Safes are my specialty, so it was an easy gig - I just walked in there pretending to be a temp, took a desk, and hid in a bathroom when everyone went to lunch. Went back in, took the stick along with some petty cash to throw them off, and then I bailed."

"What was on the data stick?"

"I don't know."

"Come on, Ali, don't bullshit me."

"I'm not." I shrink away from him a little. "Why would I lie? Don't you think I want out of this? To get away from *you*? All I want is a clean slate and a safe life for Luna and me. Roxy too. I wouldn't have taken that stupid job if I wasn't desperate. So *you* can go right ahead and just fuck yourself."

Leo frowns. He wants to say something but doesn't. After a pause, he continues with his line of questioning, ignoring my outburst.

"So someone is presumably worried about some important information getting out, but that doesn't explain the hit on you. Even if you're dead, the data stick is still out there… wait." He shoots me a look. "Do you still have it?"

"No. A guy I know put me onto the job, and when I was done, I gave it to him, and he paid me."

Leo rubs his face with his palm as he tries to think. "So this cunt who paid you to steal the data, he's trying to get rid of you? Remove the people involved? I'll pay him a visit."

I shake my head. "Mooky might know something, but he isn't high up anywhere. You said only important people could go to the *komissiya* and hire you. And besides, I've known him a long time. He wouldn't do something like that to me."

I realize I've said the wrong thing. Leo's handsome face is marred with an ugly sneer.

"Do you have any idea what I've done to myself for you, Ali?" he says. "I've turned my back on everything that mattered to me. Everything I've earned, my dues - hell, my fucking *life*. And for what? For you to tell me you don't want your little boyfriend murdered?"

I don't like his tone or his words. I stand up and set down my glass, backing away. He doesn't move.

Fuck him. I decide to stand my ground.

"I didn't *ask* you to do anything," I say. "You were safe and cherished in my memory, Leo. There, you could be anything. Then you come back, and my life is in danger. You wrench me away from my baby. And worst of all, you turn out to be everything I despise and fear in this shitty life, instead of the man I—"

"*What*, Ali?" Leo is on his feet, closing the space between us. "The man you *what*?"

It's not love. It was a fantasy. He's the father of my child, and I wanted to keep him in my heart, but now he's here, the reality is too horrific to bear.

All the fear and emotion of the last few hours suddenly spill over. I mean to slap him, but my fingers curl up tight, and I jab my fist at Leo's jaw. The punch connects with bone, and he growls, catching my fist as I try to pull it back. His other hand flies to my throat.

"You wanna fight me, *tigritsa*? Let's do it."

He walks me backward until my shoulders hit the wall. His breath is hot and harsh on my face as he presses his body against mine, pinning me in place. His hand closes around my neck, enough for me to feel his strength but not so much that it hurts.

"I hate you," I whisper.

Leo chuckles. As he leans in to lick my lower lip, I try to bite him.

"You see this?" He shifts his index finger from beneath my jaw, waggling it. I notice the Band-Aid. "*This* is where you hurt me. I tried to let it heal. But I keep opening it up."

My fingers are trying to prise away his grip on my throat, but it's impossible. He holds my other hand in his, winding our fingers together as he pins it to the wall above my head. I feel his cock digging into my thigh, and my core pulses in response.

Goddamnit.

Leo kisses my forehead, a surprisingly tender gesture.

"I didn't want to heal. I wanted to keep the pain, to keep bleeding for you. Ali, I never got over you. I tried to stay away, but fate dragged me here."

His words crash over me like a tsunami.

That's an obsession. It's unhealthy. Sick.

"And now I've got you back," he murmurs, "I'll fucking destroy anyone who tries to hurt you."

I'm afraid. Of him, of the situation. I feel like I'm going crazy. But as his fingers grip my throat, as he grinds his hard cock against me, I remember how I felt the first time. The euphoria that comes from not thinking and just *feeling*.

With that, the last bastion of my resistance is crushed.

His lips graze my ear, and I shudder. He lets go of my hand, dropping it at my side as he takes hold of my hip, pulling me toward him.

"You want me, don't you?" he says.

My body replies for me, my hand reaching for his waistband, and he laughs. "Not so fast, baby. You're mad at me, right?"

I nod as best I can with his hand wrapped around my neck. Leo reaches between my legs, pushing the thin fabric of my yoga pants against my pussy with his fingertips.

"I wanna see how you fuck angry, *tigritsa*." He pushes harder, the material dampening as he slides his fingers along my slit. "I'll sit on the bed," he tips his head at the California king against the opposite wall, beside the couch, "and you can come and do what you will. Cut me, hit me, break me, and I'll take it all. I owe you that much. All I ask is that you fuck me."

He lets go of my neck and steps backward. I draw a deep breath, my throat stinging as I realize just how tight a grip he had on me.

He sits on the edge of the bed, and I could die at the sight of him. He's so utterly uninhibited, his erection tenting his sweats as he leans back on his elbows.

I walk to the table and pick up the short dagger, keeping my eyes fixed on Leo's. He doesn't flinch.

He's fucking *serious*.

Despite everything, my pussy is soaked, a wet patch forming at my crotch.

I'm gonna have this - have *him* - and to hell with the consequences.

He said it himself - I'm probably dead already. *Why hold back?*

I stand at the foot of the bed, knife in hand, and hold the tip against my pussy. I pinch a fold of material away from my skin and nick it with the knife, making a hole in the fabric right over my slit. Leo lets out a low moan.

"What do you want, *tigritsa*? C'mon, baby. Give it to me."

I climb onto his lap, straddling him. I press the cold flat of the blade to his nipple, and he hisses through his teeth as my wet pussy soaks onto his cock through his sweatpants. I shove him in the chest to make him lie flat on his back and crawl up, so I'm on all fours, my pussy hovering over his face.

He swipes his tongue over my clit, and I nearly come there and then.

Damn. I didn't know what this was doing to me, but Leo sees my reaction.

I turn around to face his feet and sit back on my heels. He holds my ass in both hands and shimmies down a little so he can do his thing.

It's a good job he's holding onto me. As his tongue dips into my hot pussy, I nearly fall on my face.

He feels so good, sucking my clit through the fabric. With a grunt of frustration, he slides his fingers into the torn crotch and rips it wider, exposing my entire pussy and ass to his attention. He slips two fingers into me, and I grind, riding his hand as he massages my clit with his thumb.

"You're fucking wild," he says, his voice muffled as he works me with his mouth. "And so wet. You like fucking my face?"

"Shut up and eat me," I gasp. I still have the knife in my hand, and I lean forward to trail the dull side along Leo's flank. His cock lurches in response, and he groans against my sex.

"Cut me when you come," he says. "Just a little. You can mark me because I'm yours. You know that, right?"

My climax is already building, my pussy spasming around his fingers. His words push me across the threshold, and I flip the knife, pressing the sharp edge against his hip. A thin crimson line appears, a slow trickle of blood running onto the bed linen, and I drop the knife on the bed as I come, gushing onto Leo's face as he laps up my juice.

I can't move for a moment. Then Leo's hands on my ass spur me on, and I follow his lead as he turns me to face him. He sits up, his back to the headboard, and reaches behind me, freeing his cock. It's hot and wet as he bumps his hips, sliding between my ass cheeks.

"Ride me like you hate me, Ali."

11

Leo

I slide my hand to the source of the pain, feeling my blood warm on my skin.

Ali reaches for the hem of her tank top and pulls it up, taking her bra with it, and her beautiful tits are naked before me.

I didn't mean to get out of control. There's no time. I'm supposed to be saving her. Or killing her.

But I haven't touched another woman in the three years since our one night together. She's been killing *me* every day. I have to make her mine like I'm hers, or I'll go out of my fucking mind.

I know I'm sick. But she makes me embrace my sickness and revel in it in a way I didn't know was possible. Even my twisted dreams, where I fucked Ali every which way, were nothing compared with this.

There's something in me *she* needs, too. She wants to hate me, but she can't. Even though she believes I'm rotten to the fucking bone.

Her ass is lubed with her wetness, my cock slipping easily along the cleft. I grab the base of my shaft and slide against her entrance, the tip getting some purchase.

So tight. I forgot just how tiny her pussy is. I nudge further into her, and she grits her teeth as she settles her body into position, sitting back until I'm buried to the hilt. She closes her eyes and grips the top of the headboard with both hands, her nipples grazing my chest.

"This is ridiculous," she whispers. I get the feeling she's talking more to herself than to me.

I use my hand to gather some of the blood that runs down my side. Reaching up to her face, I rub my bloodied fingers over her lips. Her eyes fly open as her tongue reaches for it, licking it away before she can stop herself.

"You're depraved," she says.

The knife is beside us. I pick it up and throw it on the floor.

"Fuck *me*. You look hot with my blood on your face." I bump my hips, drawing a gasp from her. "I know what I am, *tigritsa*. It's *you* who's still fighting it. Now give me what you've got."

She takes a deep breath and flexes her thighs, rising up and off my cock. I have an incredible view as she moves along my length, her pussy clenching around me as she shifts. She picks up speed, smashing her ass into my legs, and I thrust to meet her, enjoying her slick tightness on my cock.

I have to come, but I want another one from her first. I want to see her face this time.

She throws her head back as I place the pad of my thumb on her clit, rubbing it firmly as she rides me. She looks like some mythological creature, a siren that fucks idiots to death.

"Look at me and fucking *come*, Ali," I say.

She opens her eyes and stares at me as she fucks me, panting hotly. I rub her clit more insistently and feel the deep spasms in her abdomen.

My hand shoots out and clutches her throat, yanking her toward me so I can kiss her. She screams into my mouth as she comes, her clutching wetness drenching me and tipping me into my own climax. I snarl as I pump her full of my come, my cock convulsing inside her clinging cunt.

She rests her forehead on mine as she recovers, her breathing slowing down. I run my fingertip gently over her collarbone, reassuring her.

"It's okay, Ali. You're alright. *We're* alright."

I extract myself from her and roll her gently off me and onto the mattress. She pulls the duvet over her body but doesn't speak. I lie down and face her, stroking her neck gently. I see the reddish blooms where my fingertips have marked her skin, and I touch my lips to each one. She lies motionless, her eyes closed.

"Why are you trying so hard to hate me, Ali?" I ask.

"You're an assassin," she whispers. "A man who kills people for money, with no thought or care for the pain he causes. You say you're mine? What does that mean?"

I consider the question for a moment. It's simple, but the answer isn't clear to me.

My feelings for her are consuming me, and I don't fucking like it.

"For the slimmest possibility of saving your life, I'm willing to die. Is that not fucking good enough?"

"And Luna?"

"If I'd known about her before now, I'd have taken care of you back then."

Ali's eyes widen, and I realize she's missed my meaning. "Jesus. Not like that. I mean, I would have made sure you had what you needed. I could have brought you home with me, married you."

Ali closes her eyes. The adrenaline is dumping out of her system, and sleep is finally almost upon her. She speaks quietly, her words slurred.

"I don't get it, Leo," she mumbles. "Why do you even care?"

I brush her hair off her face.

"Because you made me fucking *feel*," I whisper. "One kiss, one touch, and I was lost."

She sighs, but she's gone. Her shoulders rise and fall evenly as consciousness slips away.

Now that I'm sure she can't hear me, I say it aloud.

"You gave me a heart to lose, *tigritsa*. And I will never forgive you."

The sun is now up on what will surely be the last day of my life.

The early morning haze is lifting, but there's a chill in the air, and my sweat is cool on my skin.

I slide the door closed. It clicks, but Ali doesn't stir. She crashed out hard.

My cell phone sits in my palm. I look at it like it's an unexploded bomb.

No choice here. I have to tell Pavel what I know. He won't be happy, but he's the only person in the world I trust with this.

I find his name and dial.

"Tell me this is your check-in call, Leo." Pavel sounds like he's already been up for hours. Maybe he has.

I want to say something else. Anything to delay the moment when I let him down. He and I only have each other, and what I'm about to tell him puts him in a fucking lousy position.

Fuck it.

"Pavel, I can't kill the mark."

The silence is so cold that I half-expect my phone to freeze in my hand.

"Yes, you can," he says.

"I *won't*, then. Take your pick. But this woman isn't gonna die by my hand."

"You fucking *idiot*, Leo." Pavel snaps. "This world is full of pussy, and you go all sappy over this one, the one whose death has been sanctioned by the fucking *komissiya*?"

"I met her three years ago. She has my child."

I hear Pavel sigh. When he speaks again, the rage has gone from his voice. "Oh, Leo, my boy. I'm so sorry. Please accept my apologies for what I said."

"Fuck apologies, Pavel," I say. I sit on the raffia deckchair, feeling the pinch as the wound in my side flexes below the patch of gauze. "I want a *solution*. Someone already took a shot at her, and I killed him. It was just a bounty hunter, one of the guys who defected from the Pushkin Bratva way back."

"That shouldn't be happening," Pavel says. "The contract is yours until sunset tonight. But either way, there's nothing I can do. She's dead."

I close my eyes, trying to resist the urge to punch something. I didn't expect anything else but hearing him say it makes it all too real.

Pavel knows what I'm thinking. "There's no way around it, Leo, and you know it. Just bringing it up will raise suspicions and put a target on both of your backs, probably on mine too. Not to mention the danger to your child. I take it there was no information in the dossier? If Ben didn't find out about it, then it's very possible no one else did either. If I go to the *komissiya* with this, it will leak out that *Volk Smerti*, my heir, has a child. A child he appears to give a shit about. You don't think that's pretty fucking dangerous?"

This is why Pavel is Pakhan. Sure, it was his birthright, but he kept his position because he's got the enviable ability to see the bigger picture.

My world is smaller than his. Mostly, I'm reduced to the view through my rifle sight.

"So what the fuck do I do?" I ask.

"If you were smart, you'd kill her and the kid and spare them all this terror. But *this* is what's been eating you. You've been losing it over the last couple of years, and this woman is the reason. So you're no longer smart because you're in love."

"I am *not* in love," I snap, "but that doesn't mean I can kill her. She's the mother of my baby. You understand that, right?"

"I understand," Pavel says, sounding pained. "My brother killed his wife and child, then himself, and I've never understood why he did it. I knew he was unhappy - my father commented on how fearful he seemed - but he didn't seek help. Now *you're* reaching out to me, and I can't do anything."

I punch the wall, grazing my knuckles.

"Any suggestions at all?" I ask.

"I have two," Pavel says. "The first is to keep this very close to your chest. I'll stall for you until tonight, but then the contract will be officially open. Anyone who wants to get paid will come for her. You're the best, Leo, but you can't kill everybody."

Yes, I fucking can, I think. *And when I run out of ammo, I'll use my bare hands.*

"My other suggestion is to try to find out who the client is. If you can convince them to call it off, that's your only chance. Killing them is the next best option, but you'd have some serious explaining to do. Now go. The clock is ticking."

A click and the line goes dead.

12

Ali

A wide-screen view, like looking through a mail slot.

My Mama's bare feet, blood pooling between her toes. Then she falls, and the impact shakes the floor.

Papa pleads. He's muffled, crying. I cover my ears, but I can't block out the sounds of him struggling. I make out the word 'devil'.

Mama's blood is flowing along the cracks in the floorboards, coming toward me. I shrink away. I don't want it to touch me.

The floor under my bed is cold. Mama looks at me through the space between the bed and the ground, just like she does when we play hide-and-seek, but her eyes don't move, and she doesn't smile. I turn away and face the wall. I squeeze my eyes closed and try not to breathe. Maybe if I try hard enough, I'll disappear.

A hand grabs my ankle and pulls me into the bright light, my head knocking painfully against the floorboards.

I'm lying in my mother's blood and I don't know who this man is but he has a gun and he's pointing it at me and I can't see my Papa help me—

My eyes fly open, and I realize the screaming is coming from me. My heart is pounding, my throat closing up, and I gasp like a fish out of water.

Then he's there. His arms around me, holding me to him. He rolls me onto my side and lies along my back, spooning me.

I can't get a hold of myself. The fight-or-flight response that has been misfiring for years is going at full throttle. But Leo's hold on me gives me something unyielding to push against.

He talks gently and calmly in my ear.

"Shh, *tigritsa*, take it easy. You're safe. I'm here."

The terrified child in me hears him, and my body slows down. I go limp in his grip and dissolve into floods of tears, rolling over so I can sob into his chest.

He doesn't say a word. He wraps his arms around me and keeps me steady as I come down. After a couple of minutes, my breathing recovers, and I lean away to look at him.

"I'm so sorry," I say, my voice weak. "I feel like such a fucking idiot."

"Did I do that?" he asks, brushing my bangs off my forehead.

"No. I have…" I wonder how to phrase it, or whether I should tell him at all, "…nightmares, I guess. It's nothing serious."

Leo's smile seems bittersweet. "This is why you're like you are, Ali. Something hurt you terribly. I know it when I see it."

"What about you? I know nothing about your life."

He frowns. "There's very little to tell. My father died when I was fifteen in some fucking stupid turf dispute between the brothers of the Pushkin Bratva. My mother died when I was born and my father blamed me—his death was no great loss. I was on the streets and fell in with the Gurin Bratva because all boys want to play soldiers. Pavel Gurin gave me a gun, I went off to train, and when I came back, I took up my current vocation."

I touch his chest, placing my palm on his wolf tattoo. "Must be tough, having no family."

"I have Pavel. He's like a father to me and wants me to take over from him. Enter a loveless marriage, sire an heir. All that standard Bratva stuff."

Before I can stop myself, I imagine it—Leo, Luna, and I, as a family. I can't see *Volk Smerti* with a white picket fence, yet the thought won't fade.

He's here, ready to die for me. If - *if* - we can survive this, maybe it could work.

"What happened to you, Ali?" Leo asks. "Why do you have panic attacks? What is the nightmare that keeps coming back for you?"

I close my eyes so he can't see into my splintered memory.

I can't talk about it. Not now. I don't even remember all of what happened, but it comes back in pieces.

I twist my bracelet around my wrist.

A professional killer.

That's what the detective said when he visited me in the hospital.

A contract hit. Miracle the girl survived. The bullet grazed her head but had she not moved at the last moment, she'd have been killed rather than knocked out.

I drifted in and out of consciousness for days. Heard words I didn't understand.

Surface wound. Shock. Trauma. Psychosomatic mutism.

When the detective came, I wouldn't speak to him. I couldn't. A week later, a lady came to take me to the children's home. All I had was my pajamas and the bracelet my Mama gave me.

The bracelet is an antique with a secret locket compartment containing the only pictures I have of my parents. When our apartment was robbed, I thought it was gone forever until I saw it six months later on the society pages, draped from the slim wrist of Mrs. Moira Coffey, the senator's wife. I couldn't believe it. It must have changed hands a few times.

I thought she would be wearing it at her husband's fundraiser, but she wasn't. It was just dumb luck that it was in the safe in their room. I put the bracelet on my arm and never removed it again.

On that night - the night I met Leo - my past and my future collided.

And now that he's in my life again, everything is returning to haunt me.

How can I be falling for a hitman? The same kind of man who killed my parents and left me alone in the world, the man who is bringing all my fears home to roost?

"I don't want to talk, Leo," I say. "Just let it go."

He pulls me closer, his heart beating steadily against mine, and a dim ember inside me catches, the glow warming me.

We can make it.

"I'm gonna talk to this friend of yours," Leo says.

"Mooky." I sigh. "Okay, but I'm coming with you."

"I don't think that's wise, Ali." Leo is on his feet, pulling on a shirt.

"You said it yourself - I'm the target." I take some jeans from my holdall and tug a camisole over my head. "So I'm sticking with you. Besides, you don't know where you're going, and unless you agree I can come with, I'm not going to tell you."

Leo puts his pistol in its holster and sheaths a dagger in his ankle holster. He holds a blade out to me.

"Keep it in the scabbard and tuck the whole thing through your belt loop," he says. "Can I trust you with that?"

I smile. "You owe me a knife, anyway. You threw mine away, and I never got it back."

"Ah, yes." He frowns, then laughs. "Wait a minute. You stole my fucking car. That means *you're* in hock to *me*."

"What car do you want?"

"An Aston Martin Vantage with a fucking massive engine. Ideally red."

"And we're gonna die today?"

Leo looks anguished. "Very fucking likely."

I take the knife from him.

"I'll make you a deal. I'll buy you one tomorrow. How about that?"

～

Leo

Ali is talking to Luna on a video call.

It's hard to concentrate on driving. I want to watch their interaction and drink in the love between them.

I never had any of this. Pavel has always been good to me, but I was fifteen when my father died, and I was already an angry, difficult little prick. I ran with another messed-up kid, Kal Antonov, who lost his father in the same attempted coup that killed mine. The *Spetsnaz* straightened us both out, but when I came back, Pavel set me up as his assassin, and I never saw much of my one friend after that.

Ali is listening to Luna as she talks. She's only young, so her words aren't clear to me, but Ali repeats and reinforces everything she says, helping her learn.

"Mumma, got crispies," Luna says.

Roxy speaks up in the background. "She's trying to tell you she's been eating Rice Pops. If she says she stayed up after you left last night and watched Fishy Gets Lost, she's a liar."

Ali laughs. "Well, of course. You're a responsible adult. You'd never let that happen." Her voice cracks a little towards the end of her sentence, and I glance at her. Her eyes are shining.

"Rox," she says, "if I need you to, will you look after Luna? Like for always?"

There's a pause. I keep my eyes fixed on the road ahead. This feels intensely personal, and I wish I could give them privacy, but I can't.

"Of course I will," Roxy says, trying to keep her voice upbeat. "But Ali... you're gonna be okay, aren't you?"

"Y'okay, Mumma?" Luna asks, her baby hands large on the camera as she grasps Roxy's phone. Ali touches Luna's little fingers on the screen.

"I'm fine, baby girl," she whispers. "Mumma will be fine."

"Keep me updated," Roxy says, wrangling the phone back. "Please be careful. I'm so scared for you."

Ali hangs up without saying goodbye. She turns her head away from me, and I see her shoulders shake as she cries silently into the crook of her elbow.

She's so strong for our daughter. I didn't understand before, but I'm starting to see how much she's hurting.

"Tell me about Luna, Ali," I say.

She turns her head to look at me.

"I wish you could get to know her," she says, rubbing her face with the sleeve of her coat. "She's such a wonderful little girl. So bright and happy. Without her, I don't know if I'd have lasted this long." She starts to cry again. "And she's gonna be an orphan, just like you and me."

I don't think she meant to tell me she doesn't have her parents. I want to seize on the information and make her tell me more, but I know it's the wrong thing to do.

"I know you couldn't reach me, Ali, but tell me something - if you could have told me about Luna, would you?"

She sniffs. "Honestly? No. I had no idea who you were, but you really fucking got to me, Leo. It scared me. I told myself I didn't look for you for Luna's sake, but it was for *mine*."

"And now?" I pull into the lot beside the address Ali gave me. "You know who I am. You know how I feel about you. If we make it to tomorrow, what then?"

She leans toward me and touches my face before pulling away.

"I never forgot about you, Leo. We have something real, but it's kinda messed up too. You know it, and so do I. But I'm so fucking scared."

I smile at her.

"You're scared, Ali, but you're not a coward. You're fighting for yourself, for Luna. Instead of hiding and letting your fate come to you, you're here with me with your hair a mess and a knife tucked in your Levis, ready to throw down. It's sexy as fuck. I don't regret a second I spent longing for you."

13

Leo

The place looks like an industrial unit, but it's a brothel.

"It used to belong to the Bartanov Bratva, but their new Pakhan closed it down because flesh-for-cash isn't his bag," Ali tells me as we walk down a narrow corridor. "It's now being run by and for law enforcement. They catch a girl soliciting, and she either gets sent down for real or comes here to serve the community, so to speak."

"So this is what Mooky is into?"

"He's an informant. He's been in it for a long time, but he's still just a street rat at heart. Because his connections have improved over the years, he knows things and works as a middleman between people like me and the higher-ups who need jobs."

I look around. To my disgust, there's a Christmas tree near the door. Who is trying to create a festive atmosphere here?

There are doors off the corridor, with women working in each room, servicing corrupt cops and members of the judicial system. I wonder how many of their regular customers I've killed over the years.

A bulky man with an eye patch stops us at the top of a metal staircase, jabbing a semi-automatic weapon into my chest.

"Back up, Henchman Number One," I say. "Do you have a name? Or are you destined to be shot during a dramatic set piece?"

"Shut up," Ali hisses, tapping the gun. "It's alright, Igor. He's with me. I wanna talk to Mooky for a minute."

Igor looks from Ali to me before barking something into a radio. A crackle of static and a few muffled words in reply seem to satisfy him, and he stands aside, letting us onto the stairs.

"That's his fucking *name*?" I ask as we descend. "Jesus."

The stairwell takes us into a large basement room. The floor is covered with cushions and mattresses, and on every surface lie the prone bodies of junkies. There must be thirty people on the floor, listless and pasty. Weed smoke hangs in the air, and house music plays on a Bluetooth speaker. In the center of the carnage is an oversized corner couch facing a ninety-inch TV set. Three men sit with their backs to us, playing Mario Kart.

"Whaddayawant, Ali Cat?"

The speaker doesn't turn to look at us.

Enough of this shit. Fucking stoner asshole thinks he's a kingpin?

"*I* want something, not her," I say.

A face turns to me, his face splitting into a shit-eating grin. His teeth are crumbling, and his skin is pock-marked with scabs, both dead giveaways of a long-term meth habit. His hair is buzzed to the scalp, and I see he has dots tattooed on his forehead. Someone held him down for that; it's an old-school Russian prison mark, which means he's a snitch. No wonder he's here rather than working for a Bratva family.

"And who the fuck are you, pretty boy?" he asks. "You her boyfriend or somethin'?" He turns his attention to Ali. "You're breakin' my heart, baby."

I want to kill him. I want to fucking jump over that couch and stomp on his throat until he's gargling blood and foam.

But I need information from him. And this shit is not my forte. I'm not a negotiator. I find myself hoping he doesn't cooperate so I can rid the Earth of this grubby, parasitic little cunt.

"It doesn't matter who I am," I say. "What matters is that you tell me what I need to know. Let's keep it simple, alright, Mooky?"

Mooky glares at me before beckoning us over, waving us to sit as though we're old friends. He's flanked by two guys, neither caring to greet us as we join them on the couch.

"I need to know who gave you the job to steal the data stick," Ali says. Mooky hands her a control pad.

"Wanna play? You can be the princess if you like."

"No, I don't." She pushes the pad away, and he scowls before returning to his game. "*Please*, Mooky."

"You're in some trouble now, huh?" Mooky says, never taking his eyes off the screen. "I offered you a place to stay, Ali. You could have come here, worked a little. Brought your friend along, even. I know she's kinda innocent, but my clients like that."

Don't do it. Let her handle it. She knows him. I don't.

"Don't be a prick," Ali says. "You know I have a kid to look after."

"You wouldn't be the first whore with a brat. And apparently," Mooky nods at me, "you jumped on the first dick to come along when I've been trying to get mine wet with you for *years*. What kind of stupid bitch gives it away for free when you could have—"

I spring to my feet before I can stop myself. The guy beside Mooky tries to rise, and I slash his throat with the blade I didn't even realize I'd drawn from the ankle holster. I sock Mooky in the face good and hard to subdue him.

The man on the other side manages to punch me, making me drop my knife, but he isn't strong enough to head me off. I grab him by his hair and push his face into the upholstery before putting a cushion over his head. Pressing my knee between his shoulder blades, I shoot through the cushion and into the back of his head. The man stops moving instantly. I place my foot on the whimpering Mooky, my gun pointed at his balls.

Ali is frozen in place. I watch her, worried she's gonna lose it again. Her hands grip the seat, and her skin pales, but she gets past it.

Mooky is already babbling.

"It was Benedikt, the fixer who works for Pavel Gurin? He arranges lots of these gigs and makes himself some extra cash on the side. He gave the job to me, and I gave it to Ali. I don't know anything else about it. When I got the data stick from Ali, I paid her and kept my cut."

Holy shit. Ben organized the theft.

He has no authority to ask the *komissiya* to sanction a hit against anyone. So either his client wants Ali dead to remove a loose end, or the person whose information she stole is out for her blood.

I'll have to take this straight to Ben. I don't trust the cunt at all, but he's not in a good position to lie to me about who he's working for because when Pavel finds out he's been skimming, he's gonna get a fucking kicking.

It still feels wrong. But it's all I have to go on.

"What is he talking about, Leo?" Ali asks.

I kneel and jam the butt of my gun into Mooky's eye.

"If you know anything else, now's the time to mention it."

"I don't know, man." Mooky won't look at me, drool streaming down his face as he panics. "The less I know, the better. Why would he tell me shit? Everyone knows I'm a rat."

"You know what I do with rats?" I ask.

He opens his eyes and looks at me.

"Don't kill me. I'm sorry I said that shit to Ali."

I look at Ali, my eyebrows raised. She shakes her head, but I'm not asking.

A muffled shot and Mooky is gone.

~

"Ben, you're in serious shit."

Ben has the nerve to sound surprised. "What the fuck is your problem now?" he asks, his voice tinny and too loud in the phone speaker.

Ali sits opposite me, picking at her club sandwich.

She's been quiet since we left Mooky's place. I shot Igor on the way out, but that was it - no battle, no more guards, no nothing. It was ludicrously easy, and we just walked out of there and drove away. I don't know what to make of it, but Mooky was nobody's friend and didn't have many people willing to put their necks on the line for him.

I pick up the phone from the diner table and walk outside. I can see Ali through the window and keep my eye on her as I talk, but she doesn't need to hear this.

"Who gave you the job to have the USB stick stolen?" I ask. "Don't fuck about. I know it was you because your little errand boy snitched on you without hesitation just before I shot him."

Ben laughs. "Mooky is - *was* - a fucking moron," he says, "and to be honest, you did me a favor. But don't come to me all hot and heavy with your accusations. We're not playing *Clue*. You wanna know who set me on it? It was *Pavel*."

I breathe a sigh of relief.

This is excellent news. I already know the hit has nothing to do with Pavel, but if he arranged the theft, he knows who Ali stole from and why. And that's the information I need if she and I are to survive this.

"You'd better be telling me the truth, Ben," I say. "Because I'm gonna call him and check right now."

"I'm not fucking stupid," he snaps. "Pavel will tell you the same thing. He told me about you and your illegitimate kid. What a turn-up *that* is. You think the *komissiya* will still think you're a safe pair of hands?"

I seethe. *Fucking prick*. And why did Pavel tell him? I know he trusts Ben, but I don't, not anymore. This is what I get for keeping my thoughts to myself.

"Just keep your mouth shut," I say. "It's the anniversary of Bogdan's death tomorrow. Pavel is not in a good place, and if you cared about him as I do, you'd be supporting him, not rattling cages and trying to gain advantages you haven't earned."

"You don't care about anyone or anything. You wanted to lead the Bratva and chose to play the long game. But sometimes cutting corners means avoiding the sharp edges." I hear the sneer in Ben's voice. "And look at us now. You're out there, letting him down. I'm here at his side."

I hang up and search out Pavel's number, but a thought occurs to me, and I cancel the call before he answers.

I need to talk to him alone, and the only way to guarantee that is to visit him. He'll be at home today, preparing for the memorial wake. Better that I show up as he's not gonna want to see me, and if he thinks I'm coming, he'll try to stop me.

I go back inside. Ali is finishing her coffee, but she's hardly eaten a thing.

"You need to keep your strength up," I say, pointing at her plate. "Bring the rest of that with you."

"I don't want it," she says quietly. She looks at me as I sit down. "Why did you shoot Mooky? Those other guys, too. You killed four people and then ate a cheeseburger like it was nothing."

"It *was* nothing." I smile at the waitress as she takes my plate away, and Ali glares at me.

"It's one thing to kill someone in self-defense…"

"Ali, for fuck's sake," I say. "This is who I am. *What* I am. I haven't lied to you. Don't start with the sanctimonious bullshit just because it's happening before your eyes. Mooky insulted you, so I murdered the cunt. Everyone else was just in my way. If you're looking for my conscience, you're gonna be looking for a fuck of a long time."

I regret this little speech instantly. But I keep hearing that I'm an idiot for caring, and now Ali is sitting here judging me for not caring. I'm fucked either way.

"Oh, great," Ali says, throwing her napkin onto the tabletop. "Just when I was thinking there was more to you."

What pisses me off most is not that she believes I have nothing to offer her. It's that she's got a point. I don't fucking care at all that I killed those guys. I don't care about their families, hopes, dreams, or potential - all of that can suck my dick. They were impeding me from getting something done, so I disposed of them, and I don't feel any kind of way about it.

I have strong feelings about killing Mooky, but only because he dared to speak to Ali that way. I'd love to kill the fucker all over again.

My cell phone rings, and I see it's Pavel calling me back. I cancel the call and get to my feet.

"I gotta follow something up, but I need you out of the way. I'll take you back to the apartment."

14

Ali

"I don't want to stay here, Leo. I told you. And you told *me* I'm not safe alone."

Leo isn't listening to me. He's looking through binoculars at the buildings nearby.

"Stop fucking doing that and *listen* to me!"

I grab a cushion from the bed and throw it at him. He catches it out of the air without even looking away from the window.

"Ali, I'm checking for watchers. Someone already tried to attack you, and the contract expires in," he checks his watch, "just over six hours. I don't have time to argue the details with you. I said you can't risk Luna's life by staying with her, but no one knows you're here."

"What makes you so sure?"

He's still not paying attention. He's all business now, his assassin training taking over.

He thinks he cares about me, but I wonder what that would involve day-to-day.

Men want what they want. He's decided it's me he wants to obsess over, but why? I'm nobody. The real Ali may fall a long way short of the dream vision he held in his head over the years. Even if we make it, he might realize that I'm not worth everything he gave up for me, and then what?

The one warm spot in his icy heart, the place he keeps for me, might freeze forever.

And I don't want *Volk Smerti*. I want *Leo*.

I think about what he said earlier about marriage and an heir. Does he know how to love? Has anything in his world prepared him for what it really means to *be* with someone?

I don't want to think about what it means if the answer is no. Because if Leo doesn't honestly care - if he isn't capable of it - then Luna and I would be in tremendous danger. How much would it take for him to lose his shit and murder *us*? He killed today over little more than a few rude words.

"Will you tell me what's going on?" I ask. "I think I'm entitled to know."

"I'm not telling you shit. The less you know, the better."

I have had enough.

"This is *my* life at stake, Leo. I don't have it in me to carry on this way. You think I'm strong, but I'm not—"

Leo is before me in an instant. He holds my face in both hands, cupping my chin. I feel his warmth as he rests his forehead against mine.

"Look at me, *tigritsa*." His turquoise eyes seem almost luminous. "You are a warrior. I don't know what happened in the past, and I don't want to drag it out of you - you'll tell me in your own time." He kisses me gently. "I was like you once, and I closed my heart and shut down my feelings to cope. But you? You're *way* fucking braver than me. You let yourself *feel* it, held onto it, and that's why you're such an incredible mother. Because you refused to allow the pain to kill your capacity for love."

I didn't know he saw this in me. Is this why he brings out that raw, desperate side whenever he touches me? Because he understands my heart?

"Tell me you'll stay," he whispers, stroking my cheek. "Tell me you'll stay here while I do what I must."

"I'll stay. But I need you," I say, melting into him. "You frightened me today. I don't want to be afraid."

"Yes, you do." Leo's caressing hand slides down, massaging my throat gently. "But differently. Fighting me, fucking me. Hurting me while I hurt you. It makes you feel alive."

"Yes," I whisper. "I don't understand it."

"Me neither. But it's the same for me. No one else ever made me feel like you do, Ali."

He picks me up with one arm and sets my ass on the kitchen countertop, pressing his body between my legs. I find myself wishing he'd grip my neck a little more firmly, and like magic, he obliges. His hand is large enough to provide pressure without cutting off my air supply, and I simmer with lust at how possessive and wrong it feels to be held that way.

"Be a good girl and do what I tell you?"

Oh my God, yes. My demons can't burn me up if we make a fire bigger than anything they can raise. Put your hands on me and set me alight.

"I'll be good," I say.

Leo crushes his lips to mine in a feverish kiss, his tongue delving into my mouth. He bites my lip, and I groan, already craving the nasty I know he has for me. He fumbles at my zipper, releasing my neck so he can peel my jeans halfway down, taking my panties with them.

"Hold your legs up so I can see your pussy."

I grab my thighs and lean back, exposing my sex to his gaze. My jeans are holding my legs together, my plump pussy lips and rosy asshole lewdly on display. He runs his fingertip through my slit, using my wetness to lubricate my tightest hole.

"I'm gonna fuck you in the ass, Ali," he says. "That wasn't what I was planning, but now I gotta do it."

I balk, tensing instinctively.

"I've never done that before," I whisper. "Does it hurt?"

He laughs, dragging more of my pussy juice onto my asshole and massaging it over my tender flesh. "I've never been on the receiving end, baby, so I can't comment. But it's okay. That's not the kind of pain we like. I'll take it steady."

I'm barely taking in what he's saying. His fingertip has breached the tight ring of muscle at my opening, and he's sliding his finger slowly in and out, my natural lubrication flowing from my pussy and easing his movements. It feels incredible, and my pussy throbs jealously.

"Touch yourself, Ali. I wanna watch you do it, and it'll make it easier for you to take me."

My clit leaps at the slightest touch. I slip my fingers between the slick lips of my pussy, cradling my clit between them, and sigh with pleasure.

"You want a little something?" Leo asks. His voice is thick with lust. "Because I wanna slap the hell out of that pink pussy of yours. It's so fucking slutty, getting so wet for me just because it's your ass getting the attention."

He withdraws his finger from my asshole, and I moan from the loss. He leans onto my legs, folding me in half to get a good angle. A quick glance at my face confirms I want it.

Fuck, I want it. My pussy is pulsating with need, my fingertips working my swollen clit.

I want to feel *more*. Agony, ecstasy - it's all the same. There could never be too much. Not with Leo.

He raises his hand and brings it down right on my pussy. He doesn't hold back; for a moment, I can't feel anything except a sudden and complete numbness. Then the pain flares across my sensitive core, mingled with the sublime sensations in my clit.

It's so cathartic. I could cry, but not from the pain. The feeling is so overwhelming that it overpowers everything. My fear, my trauma, it's all drowned out.

Leo sees my face and understands. He spanks my pussy again with a growl, and I cry out this time.

"Fucking *scream* for me, *tigritsa*." He hits my ass cheek with the flat of his hand, then with the back. I yelp, my pussy leaping and clutching at nothing. "Scream your throat raw. Get it all out. It's for *you*. Everything I have, everything I am, is yours."

Without warning, he plunges his fingers into my pussy, massaging my sweet spot firmly as he frees his cock. I continue to rub my clit, chasing my climax even as my flesh burns and throbs in the aftermath of Leo's firm hand.

"Are you my good girl, Ali?" I feel his cock nudging between my buttocks, sliding against my sensitive asshole. He's fingering me roughly now, his free hand reaching for me.

"I am," I cry. "I'm your good girl."

He grabs a handful of my hair and leans closer, thrusting his fingers deep. He shoves his hips, lodging the head of his cock in my ass, and I squeal.

"Look at me." He fixes his eyes on mine, but he keeps moving his hand, and I realize he's doing it deliberately to keep me right on the edge.

"Don't do that," I gasp. "Leo, you fucking sick bastard. Let me come!"

"I will. But I'm gonna fuck your ass right through it. Can you handle that?"

"I don't know, and I don't fucking care!" My fingers are cramping as I chase my climax. "Just do it!"

Leo curls his fingers, and one firm thrust is all it takes. I shriek with exquisite bliss, and my pussy squirts obscenely as my climax smashes through me.

The liquid runs into the crack of my ass, coating and lubricating his cock. He's still holding my hair and looking me in the eye as he presses his weight forward, burying his cock to the hilt in my twitching ass.

"Fuck, that feels incredible," he groans, pulling back until he's nearly free of me before plunging back inside. He pulls my jeans over my ankles so he can open my legs and get deeper inside me, leaning in for a kiss as he does so. His thrusts become rougher as his mouth clashes with mine, his stubble grazing my face.

"You like me in your ass, don't you? I knew you would." I feel his cock throbbing as he moves. "Such a good slut. You're perfect, Ali."

It feels so dirty to have his cock in my asshole while he stares into my eyes and calls me a slut. Yet somehow, it's incredibly intimate.

Leo doesn't care how he looks to me. He doesn't wonder whether he's too much because he knows I can take it. Not just his cock, not just the sex he wants to give me, but him.

I can fucking *handle* him, and that makes me feel like there's nothing in this world I can't overcome.

He's buried in my ass, his fingers tangled in my hair, and now he's rubbing my sensitive clit, driving me toward another orgasm.

Too late. He presses his forehead to mine in a mirror of the loving gesture he made only minutes ago, and he holds my gaze as he comes, spurting inside my clenching ass. He pulls free with a shuddering groan, a string of semen linking us like a cobweb.

"Oh, that is fucking disgusting," he says, sounding awestruck. "I love it."

"I nearly came again," I pout. "You didn't let me get there."

"Greedy girl," Leo smiles. "You tell me what you want, baby, and I'll give it to you. I'm not gonna leave my woman hanging just because I got off already."

His woman. Despite everything, the words warm me inside. His attentiveness gives me courage, and I say it.

"Put your fingers in both my holes."

Leo's face splits into a delighted grin. "Attagirl," he says. "Come here and get comfortable."

I kneel on the edge of the bed, my legs wide and my puffy asshole on show. My pussy is still quivering, my clit pulsating gently. Leo puts his hand on my back and pushes me forward onto my hands, my ass stuck out behind me.

"Give me an image for next time I'm jerking off," he says. "Push my come out of you, Ali. I know you can do it."

I tense my muscles, feeling his hot seed spill out of my ass and run over my pussy. I can't see his face, but I hear him moan with pleasure at the sight.

He touches me, his index finger smoothing his come over my skin before pushing it back inside me. His hand brushes my pussy, and I feel his other fingers enter me.

It's so intense to feel this full. It's a nasty, lewd act, and it feels fucking incredible.

"You're squeezing me so tight," Leo says. "You wanna come? Then *do* it."

I reach for my clit again as his movements gather pace, his fingers plunging in and out of me. I feel sore and sensitized and obscenely aroused all at once.

My body convulses suddenly, and my orgasm hits me like a train. Leo jams his fingers into me, giving something to grip and spasm against as pleasure surges through my nerves. I collapse face-down on the bed, panting into the duvet as he withdraws his fingers from me.

Leo sits beside me, and I turn in time to see him licking our mingled fluids from his hand.

I grin. He's so fucking filthy, and he makes me feel like the only woman on Earth.

"What's so funny, *tigritsa*? You want some of this?"

I shriek with laughter as he reaches for me, wiping his hand on my face. He rolls on top of me and clasps my hands in his, lifting them over my head as he kisses me, the taste of our shared ecstasy on his lips.

"You're amazing," he murmurs.

15

Ali

I watch him gather himself together. A quick shower, a change of clothes, and it's like it never happened.

Except something changed. It wasn't what he did to me. It's what he said.

You are a warrior.

I never felt like a warrior. After my parents were killed, I didn't speak for three years. Nobody came for me, and no one wanted to adopt me because I was mute. I lived in that children's home until I was seven, and every night, I was beaten for screaming in my sleep. It was the only sound I made. I ran away, but when I returned cold and hungry the following morning, the Catholic nuns who ran the place wouldn't let me in. One called me a whore, but I didn't know what it meant.

The streets aren't safe for anyone, especially not children. I lived and worked in a box factory until I was twelve, but the place was raided, and all of us underage workers were turfed out to fend for ourselves. I wasn't a good thief back then, so it wasn't long before I ended up in juvie, where I learned to read, write, shoot, and steal.

Never in my life have I felt like a strong person. I wrestle with my nightmares, my flashbacks. I look for the face of the person who killed my family, but my memory has locked it away, and I can't reach it. What good would it do now to remember?

But when Leo tells me I'm strong, I believe him. Of all the hits he's carried out, all the marks he took out without a thought, I'm the only person he *ever* refused to kill. He's ruined his life for a slim chance of saving mine. If that's not love, what is it?

It's not the time to say these things out loud. But I can *think* it. I can hold it in my heart.

"Leo, what are you going to do?"

He turns to look at me, holstering his gun beneath his jacket. He's so fucking sexy, his bedhead hair tumbling over his brow as he sweeps his hand through it.

A sudden fear strikes me. *I may never see him again.*

"I'm going to talk to my boss," he replies. "Pavel. He knows who the data stick belongs to, and I need to get him alone so I can talk to him. Something doesn't add up, and he's the only person I can be certain won't bullshit me."

"So this leads back to your people? What the fuck is that about?"

"Ali, I don't know," he raises his voice in exasperation, "but I won't find out standing around here. Just stay put. I think an erstwhile friend may be trying to fuck with me, but I need more to go on before I can act."

I open my mouth to speak, but he's gone.

No kiss, no parting words. If he's afraid he won't come back, he sure as fuck isn't moved enough to share that with me. I think about opening the door and shouting after him, but I feel suddenly foolish, and I sit for a long minute, the duvet pulled over me.

I didn't want him to go without me. He said all the right things and fucked me into submission, and now he's left me behind, just as he planned.

A sickly feeling settles into my stomach. It's one I've felt before - the age-old inkling that maybe I'm being manipulated.

∽

Leo

Pavel is outside in his garden when I arrive. I didn't expect to see him out here because of how cold it is. He's sitting on the bench, a cup of Russian caravan tea in his hands.

"What the fuck are you doing here?" he asks. "It's a good job I'm keeping people away from the house today. Ben is out dealing with business for me while I make the last of the arrangements for Borden's memorial."

Yeah, I'll bet he fucking is.

I did a lot of thinking on the way over.

I suspect Ben knew about Ali and me. He compiled the dossier on her - I don't know how he found out that Luna is my child, but he did somehow. The man is a master information miner; if anyone knows, he'll find out. He's contrived a way to get a hit put out on her knowing I wouldn't do it, thinking it's a way to get rid of me and ensure his own ascendency to the Bratva leadership.

It's a trap.

I have no proof of this. Pavel is not my biggest fan right now, and Ben will indeed be looking good, given that, as things stand, I'm a dead man walking.

"I have some shitty news," I say. "Ben has been skimming the top off the jobs you give him."

Pavel frowns. "I expected that. Everyone is on the take, Leo. If you were Pakhan, you'd learn that."

I notice the choice of words. He said 'if' not 'when.' The old man has counted me out of the game.

"It's not why I'm here, anyway. Ben gave a job to a guy he knows called Mooky, and that guy outsourced it again to Ali - *my* Ali. A USB data stick. She lifted it and gave it to her guy. I assume it made it into your hands?"

Pavel frowns. "Yes. At least into Ben's. As you say, I just pass this shit on."

"What's so important about the disc?"

"It's part of a little game I have going with Senator Coffey," Pavel says, sipping his tea. "You know the rumors in Washington, the ones The Tattler got sued over? All true. I've patronized the bastard for years, kept his campaign funds topped up, you know."

Senator Coffey is said to have a thing for young girls. Really young girls. A few years ago, he was just into hookers, but when he realized that the only limit was money, he let his natural proclivities out to play.

"So Coffey got mouthy," Pavel continues. "Wanting more, offering less. He didn't do a thing to help when Judge Brazier fucked us up way back. When you killed the judge, the senator got scared for a while, but recently he's been at it again. I heard he was dumb enough to have his latest jailbait sex party filmed, so I figured it might tip the scales in my favor if I got hold of that footage. He kept it in his wife's office safe like a moron. Who does that?"

"So Coffey is not just a pedophile," I say. "He's also a liability. How does a man like that reach his station in life?"

Pavel shrugs. "With the help of men like me, who need a legitimate face to represent their interests. It's dirty, but isn't everything? The senator doesn't know I have the data stick, but he's scared. He told me he had footage of the person who stole it from his office security camera, and I told him to take it to Ben to see if he could identify the thief, but that's the last I heard of it until now. Coffey thinks I'm trying to help him, so he's back in my pocket, and he still thinks we're buddies. What a fucking idiot."

That's it.

Ben looked into it for the senator, found out about Ali's connection to me, and convinced him to put a hit on her knowing I wouldn't do it. Knowing I'd go from the King's hand to an outlaw overnight, leaving him to pick up the pieces.

Smart. But now isn't the time to deal with him. Even if I murder the conniving shit, it won't change a thing. Ali would still be the mark, and the senator would still want her dead. Better to let Ben think I haven't figured it out.

"Pavel, I'm gonna go to see Coffey and give him one chance to stand down. If he wants his fucking disgusting home movie back, can't we give it to him?"

"It's not ideal, Leo," Pavel says with a frown. "If he's gonna be alive and useful to me, I need the leverage over the cunt." He leans closer to me as he speaks. "Do yourself and me a favor and kill him. It doesn't matter how your woman got mixed up in this. All that matters is how *you* get her out of it. But you didn't hear that from me. We may yet be able to make this bullshit go away."

My Pakhan has told me to kill the person who wants Ali dead. That's job satisfaction at its best. All I have to do is take out that dirty bastard Coffey, and the *komissiya* will call off the hit. Pavel will vouch for me.

The voice in my head chooses this moment to pipe up.

Then what? You're gonna bring her and the kid home and set up house as a family? She wants peace and safety. Love. You can't offer her that and you know it.

I bat the thought away.

That's all in the future. Gotta stick to business.

I stand, and Pavel follows. He shakes my hand.

"All I want is for you to make it through this, Leo," he says. He looks weary. "I didn't expect all this trouble. It was a straightforward job. One bullet and done, like all the others. Now it's a mess."

I nod. "I know. But not for long. You can rely on me, I promise."

∽

Ali

The water feels good. I soap my body, the suds cleansing my skin.

Sweat, tears, blood, filth, come. I'm marked by myself and by Leo too.

I wonder how I got here so fast.

Leo says we're going to die, and I believe him. A familiar fatalism is settling on me like snow.

Some people would think they were blessed to survive a gunshot to the head, but for me, it always felt as though I'd cheated. Death would get around to correcting his mistake when he got a minute.

So it's ironic that when death came back for me, he couldn't finish the job. Fate handed the gun to a man who wouldn't pull the trigger.

Leo would die for me. That much, I believe. But I'm not sure he'd *live* for me. I don't know if he even wants to have a future at all, let alone share it. He says he sees my pain, but it's his own wounds he needs to attend to, and I don't mean the ones I made on his body.

I get out of the shower and wrap myself in a towel. My phone screen shows a missed call notification, and when I open it, I'm pleased to see it's Roxy. I swipe to video call.

"Ali!" Roxy cries, giving me a wave. She's outdoors somewhere, and my stomach drops.

"Where are you?" I ask, looking anxiously for my daughter in the background. "I don't see Luna. Why are you outside?"

"Leo called the hotel and told me to take Luna out someplace," she says. "We've been for ice cream and then to the toy store. No prizes for guessing what she picked out!"

She tilts her phone to reveal Luna sitting on a swing set, and I realize they're in a park. Luna is in one swing, and her new toy is in the other.

"Mumma!" Luna beams, pointing at her prize. "Got big bunny!"

We used to go to the toy store regularly just so she could hold that stuffed rabbit. It's as big as her, and I've been scrimping and saving for months to buy it for Christmas.

"It was the last one, Ali," Roxy says. She waves a credit card at the camera. "I've been swiping this baby like it's my job."

I'm so glad to see my best friend and my beloved child so happy. My heart aches that I can't be there with them.

"Thanks for everything you're doing, Rox. I miss Luna so much, but it helps a lot to see she's happy. I don't mind being alone when I know she's got you."

"Leo isn't with you?" Roxy asks. "Where did he go?"

"He's gone to speak to his boss about it all. I don't know what to make of it, and he says he's not sure either, but I think Leo is hiding something from me."

"He's a contract killer. You were his target, and you don't think he knows anything about the reason?" Roxy sounds incredulous. "I think you are right to be suspicious. He may have his own reasons for trying to save you. Since when were Bratva men - or any men - known for their chivalry? You're the mother of his child. Doesn't that make you a valuable commodity?"

This is the creeping doubt I've been trying to push down.

"It would be easier for Leo just to kill me and start again," I say. "Why would he risk his life when he could get someone else?"

"Because you already have Luna," she says. "And besides, even if I'm wrong - it's not as though he's discussed any of this with you. He knows you want a clean slate. A clean life."

"That's because he thinks we're going to die, Roxy!" I say. "So, funnily enough, we haven't had too many chats about the future!"

Luna starts to cry.

I'm an idiot. I said that too loud.

It's not even Roxy I'm angry with - it's Leo. And *myself* for getting in so deep.

Roxy picks Luna up and shows her my face.

"See? Mumma's right there. She's okay. You wanna give her a kiss?"

Luna wipes her eyes with the back of her hand, just like I do when I'm upset. Her lips loom on the screen, and I choke back a sob, turning it into a chuckle as I kiss the phone.

"Have fun with Big Bunny!" I say. Luna grins and squirms, eager to return to playing, and Roxy puts her down again.

"I'm sorry, Rox. It's all fucked up. Hang on in there."

Roxy nods and gives me a small smile. "I love you, girl. You're gonna make it, for Luna. I *know* you are."

16

Leo

Someone is fucking tailing me.

I don't know who it is, but he's gotta be hoping I'll lead him to Ali. If I don't shake him...

Fuck this. I'm not gonna try to lose the fucker. I'm gonna *kill* him. After all the bullshit, I have had enough. I'm in the mood to end someone's life.

I cut across two lanes to take a left, and the guy can't keep up. I watch in the rearview mirror as he misses the turn.

The road I'm now on rejoins the main drag via another left junction further along. If my pursuer thinks I haven't seen him, he may be stupid enough to take that route and try to head me off.

I pull over and park, turning off the engine. I open the window and take out my pistol, clicking off the safety. I'm holding it below the eyeliner of any passers-by, but luckily the road is deserted.

All I can do now is wait.

Sure enough, the car following me rounds the corner, driving toward me. The driver sees me as I raise my weapon, my arm out of the window. I see his gun in his hand.

Shots are fired, and the man's head snaps back, blood spattering over the seat. It takes me a moment to realize I'm bleeding too, a growing patch soaking my shirt sleeve below my elbow.

The moving car veers toward me, out of control, and smashes into the front right of the hood. The impact isn't severe enough to smack my head into the dash, but it whips my neck, setting off a throbbing pain in the base of my skull.

My car starts the first time. I back up slowly, pieces of broken glass falling from the crumpled hole where the headlight should be. I leave the engine running while I get out and have a look at the guy I just killed.

He's not one I recognize, but he knew me. He knew my car, my face. Now that Ben is pulling strings, the contract exclusivity is all to fuck. Anyone and everyone is looking for us.

I'm not a ghost anymore. *Volk Smerti* has a face and can bleed. Can die.

I have to get back to her.

༄

"What the fuck happened?"

Ali's eyes are wide with shock at my state. I can't blame her. Despite my efforts to stem the bleeding, my arm is still pretty bad, although the pain in my neck is abating.

She looks beautiful. How could she not? She's showered, her bangs frizzy as they air-dry, and there's not a scrap of makeup on her face.

I don't care. I want her as she is right now - natural and unadorned.

But I'm angry. My thoughts are breaking apart.

Because I love her.

I was denying it even to myself, but I know it's true. And I have to save her. What if I can't?

It's because of *me* she's in this fucking danger in the first place. If she weren't the mother of my child, Ben wouldn't have dragged her into this. He used her to get to me because he didn't have the guts to fight - he wanted to sneak around like a coward and manipulate Pavel and me.

But that doesn't mean it's not my fault.

"Someone chased me, baby. I don't know how he found me, but I spotted him in time and took him out. He got a shot off, but it's not too bad."

Ali looks dubious as I remove my jacket. The blood seems pretty bad, but I've had worse. Her fingers move to my shirt buttons, undoing them one by one. I clench my teeth and snarl as she peels the fabric away from the wound.

I was right - it's superficial. The bullet nicked my forearm but narrowly avoided any major arteries. Just as well, or I wouldn't be here. Best not to tell Ali how close a call it was.

I sit on the couch as Ali fetches the first-aid kit from under the sink. It's pretty helpful that the place was another hitman's apartment - like me, the guy has a lot of medical supplies, booze, and fuck all else.

Ali brings the whiskey bottle with her. She sits beside me and tips the alcohol onto a piece of gauze, dabbing at my injury.

"That whiskey just went from good to shit," I say through the pain. "Shame it's not Bell's after all. We may have just found something it would have been good for."

"How can you make jokes?" Ali asks. "You could have been killed."

I shrug. "That's my day job, *tigritsa*. I don't think about it."

"You have me and Luna to think about now."

We lapse into silence as she patches me up. She applies surgical wound sealant, pinching the raw edges together as it sets.

"That fucking hurts," I say, smiling at her. "Fun for you?"

She doesn't answer for a moment, and when she speaks, she tries to change the subject.

"So I called Roxy and spoke to Luna. They've been out, having fun. Shopping. And on your dime, I'm told."

"Sure." I hold the clean gauze, and she tapes it in place. "I know it hurts you not to be with our daughter. I can only do what I can to make it easier on her."

"Thank you," she says, kissing me tenderly. "It was wonderful to see Luna so happy. She has the bunny I wanted to get her for Christmas, but I couldn't afford it."

"Neither you nor Luna will want for anything ever again. If my girls want something, they will have it. I won't even question it."

"You say that like it could happen." Her shoulders sag. "But we don't have a future, do we?"

"There's a chance that'll change by tonight."

Ali raises her eyebrows. "Your boss knew something?"

"It turns out that Pavel - the Pakhan - was the one who wanted the data stick stolen. He gave the job to an associate of mine, who passed it on to Mooky, and then you were the last link in the chain. The stick has footage on it of a sex party - underage girls. Care to guess who it belonged to?"

Ali's mouth drops open. "Senator Coffey? Oh, that is so gross." She frowns. "So you're saying all this is—"

"A coincidence. Yes."

Her ignorance benefits me. I don't want to tell her about Ben's part in all this because I don't want her to know that it's me who is fucking up her life. Let her believe it's her own doing, at least until I know it's over.

"Pavel thinks I might get the *komissiya* on my side if I kill Coffey, but the important thing is that they will automatically withdraw the hit on you as there'll no longer be a client. The Bratva has no quarrel with you personally, but I'll be in the shit." I flex my arm. It feels better already. "I have to kill the senator tonight. We're almost out of time. I know a few mavericks have tried to get us, but it'll be open season after sunset."

"Only him, Leo."

I look at Ali. Her face is set and unsmiling.

"I mean it," she continues. "Do only what you have to. I can't think of you as a heartless killer. I have to believe you're better than that."

I stand up, towering over her. "*You* are my heart. I would kill anyone - *everyone* - in the fucking world for you," I say. "If I had to murder ten thousand people to keep you from getting a speck of grit in your eye, then I'd line them up without a second thought." I gesture at my bandaged arm. "I'm bleeding for you. *Again*. And I'd bleed more than this if it meant you and Luna would be safe."

I know I'm going too far, but I'm amped up and ready to have at it.

"I need us to be safe from *you*," she says, standing to face me. Though she's far shorter than I am, she's squaring up, closing the gap between us. "I appreciate everything you're doing. But I think you're hiding something from me, and that's why you're behaving this way. You think if you act out, you can distract me."

"That's what a toddler would do," I sneer. "You sure you're not thinking of Luna?"

"Don't you fucking speak my daughter's name!" Ali yells, tears springing to her eyes. She blinks hard, trying to hold on to her rage and not let fear and despair overcome her. "This is the longest I've ever gone without her. It's killing me. And now you're not telling me things and giving me shit just because I don't want the man I'm falling for to murder innocents?"

She's falling for me.

Her survival was the only goal. Nothing else mattered.

Now I want her love. If there's a shot at earning her heart, I'll take it.

I reach for her, cupping her cheek in my palm. She wants to resist, but she can't. My other hand wraps around her waist, and I pull her to my chest, feeling her tears dampen my shirt.

"It'll be alright, Ali," I say. "But I have to go. Trust me."

"What choice do I have?"

I release her from my hold and pick up my rifle case. The keys are on the countertop, and I grab them, my body blocking Ali's view.

"There's a spare pistol under the bed," I say. "Stay here, and don't contact anyone until I get back."

"Leo?"

I turn to look at her, my hand on the door handle.

"Yes, *tigritsa*?"

Ali's eyes burn with passion.

"Kill that filthy bastard for me, and come back to my arms."

This woman. I'll worship her until the day I die.

I nod. I open the door and step through it, but as I go to close it behind me, I'm struck by a cold feeling of dread.

She's looking at me, her turbulent eyes holding mine. She looks wild and angry and heartsore all at once. I drink her in, locking her into my memory.

This may be the last image I have of her.

The thought spurs me into saying the words I never thought I'd say aloud.

"I love you."

I lock the door behind me as I go.

17

One hour later…

Leo

Thank *fuck* Coffey is at home.

Does the stupid asshole still think I'm running around trying to find Ali and kill her? I don't know how much he knows. I suspect Ben convinced him to put the hit out on Ali in the misguided hope that this would send a message to whoever has his precious little homemade porno, and he's oblivious to the real reason.

I can see why Paval wanted the Senator in his pocket. A man this easy to manipulate could be a real asset. I'd feel sorry for the guy if he wasn't a child-molesting cunt, but as it is, I'm fucking delighted to murder him. He has a wife and a young son who would be much better off without him. Helpfully, they appear to be out. I don't like killing people in front of their kids if I don't have to. It's gratuitously sadistic.

The light is almost gone, and the sun is low in the sky. I'm lying in the shrubbery on the perimeter of the Coffey family's perfectly manicured front lawn, Christmas lights flashing above me where they're strung along the hedge.

I have my rifle in hand. It's the M110 semi-automatic - probably excessive for my purposes, but I'm taking no chances.

Coffey is in the kitchen, preparing food. He moves slowly as though he has the weight of the world on his shoulders. He stands at the kitchen sink, gazing out the window as he drains pasta, and for a moment, his eyes seem to meet mine. Then he moves away and sits at the breakfast bar, his back to me. He flicks on the television.

I switch on the laser sight, a tinny sound coming from it as it powers up. The red dot appears on the senator's back, and I track it up his spine, careful to keep it on his body where he won't see it.

A clean shot to the back of the neck. It's more than the piece of shit deserves.

I line it up, breathing out as I squeeze the trigger—

Coffey bends down suddenly, and the bullet flies past him, destroying the television. He looks behind him at the shattered window, blinking moronically. The fork he dropped is back in his hand.

Shit.

I roll out from under the hedge and stand up, taking the rifle with me. I brace the weapon against my shoulder and march across the lawn, the security light illuminating me as I go. Coffey sees me and hits the deck as I open fire.

The kitchen disintegrates into splinters as my gunfire decimates it. I vault over the sill and through the space where the window was. The senator tries to roll away and head for the door, but he isn't fast enough, and I wing him in the shoulder, sending him sprawling.

"I knew you'd come," he cries, blood pouring between his fingers as he grips the gunshot wound. "You're too late. Even if you kill me and the hit is called off, he'll get to her."

I drop my rifle and remove my knife from my ankle holster, pressing it to Coffey's throat.

"I will make you suffer unless you tell me what's going on," I say. "You know who Ali is? You were working with him?"

"It's not about the fucking data stick," Coffey spits, his voice throttled by pain. "He identified the girl from the security footage and saw his chance to get her. I couldn't argue because it was him who had my fucking data stick stolen in the first place. He told me you'd gone rogue and wouldn't kill the girl. After that, I knew you'd come for me."

"Why?" I press the blade, the tip making a tiny pinprick wound appear on Coffey's neck. "Why didn't you call it off? You could have gone to Paval—"

"There's nothing you can do now!"

Coffey is losing it. His skin is pallid, sweat beading on his brow as blood continues to flow from his shoulder wound. "He said he'd kill them if I tried to pull the hit. He wants her dead. She's the key to everything."

His voice is fading now. I drop the knife and grab him by his collar, slapping him across the face.

"Wake up, you fucking pervert. What do you mean, she's the key?"

"He killed them," Coffey mumbles. "Paval's family."

Coffey's eyes roll in his head, and he's gone.

Jesus fucking Christ.

Ben killed Bogdan? It's possible. Paval found him hanged, but that doesn't rule out foul play. How old would Ben have been then? Sixteen?

He came to us around that time, when I was eighteen and returning from my training. I was in Russia when Bogdan and his family died, and I never met the guy. He and Pavel were estranged long before then.

I close my eyes and rub my face with my palm, accidentally smearing blood on myself.

This shit is hurting my head. There's a crucial element missing somewhere that would make this add up, but it's elusive. If I could get space to fucking *think*...

The senator sits up, a gargling sound coming from his throat. He looks at me, his eyes widening as he registers the knife in my hand.

"Glaar!" he cries, cutting off as I swipe the sharp edge over his throat. He doesn't have enough blood spare to bleed for long, and a crimson sheet cascades down his chest for only a couple of seconds before he slumps to the ground.

Fuck. I did that without thinking. My training working against me for the first time ever.

I pull my cell phone from my pocket and call Paval.

"Is it done?" he barks.

"Coffey is dead." I open my phone camera and take a snap of the senator's body. "You can get the *komissiya* to call it off now."

Paval sighs. "I already spoke to Pushkin. Did you know he's the chair now? He handed off the leadership of his Bratva to his son-in-law, so he's semi-retired. He said he'd see that the *komissiya* would formally retract the hit on Ali, which means grave consequences and zero payment for anyone who hurts her."

"Unless it's negotiated privately," I say. "I spoke to Coffey. He confirmed my suspicions. Ben is behind this. I'm certain of it now."

I wonder whether I should tell him what Coffey said about Bogdan, but I decide against it. The old man has had a fuck-awful couple of days, partly thanks to me. It's Bogdans's memorial wake soon - it seems like a bad time to speculate about whether the poor bastard was actually murdered. It's not as though the truth will bring him and his family back.

"I don't understand, Leo," Paval says, "but I know you wouldn't make an accusation like that lightly. Ben isn't here at the moment, but once he shows up, I'll detain him and let you know."

He coughs, and I wince, wondering if I'm gonna return to find him dead and Ben crowing over his corpse.

"You need to come home, my boy. I need you here. If you're right about all this, I'll vouch for you with the *komissiya*. But hit or no hit, they will be very interested to hear your justification for blowing away a senator on your own authority."

Ali

"He locked you in?"

On the phone screen, Roxy screws up her face in disgust.

"Rox, I was angry too when I realized. But you're not listening to me. He told me he *loves* me."

"Ali, he's a professional killer. That's not a man who loves you. That's a psycho obsessed with you, and there's a difference."

I think of the dangerous, cathartic sex Leo and I had. As much as I want to blame the danger for upping the ante, it's not entirely true. Because we were like that on the night we had together three years ago.

Something in his soul speaks to mine. I'm yet to dig down into his pain, but I feel my own trauma rising to the surface.

My dreams grow ever more lucid. Memories long buried are reaching for the light, wanting to be seen and known.

I don't want to be that frightened orphan anymore. The girl who saw the people she loved die and always kind of wished she'd gone with them.

Until Luna.

When I met Leo, I was only twenty years old, cocksure, and full of bravado. I thought I was living, but I was *existing*. He gave me a beautiful gift, a reason to knuckle down and commit to being alive.

Leo reaches into me and stokes the fire that I desperately want to feel. And he is out there now, killing for me, possibly dying for me.

The man who loves me.

How can I turn that away?

"I know you're scared, babe," I say, "and so am I. But I believe in him, not just because I have to but because it's how I *feel*."

Roxy's voice is low, trying not to wake the sleeping Luna. "You've always been afraid of being abandoned again. This is the first time I've seen you show genuine faith. Do you believe Leo is your happy ending? That he's a man and not just another bad dream?"

"Yes. We're gonna make it, Rox. I think he's for real."

Roxy smiles.

I hear the key in the door.

"Gotta go," I say. I give her a wave and hang up, leaping to my feet.

The door opens, and Leo is there. He looks exhausted, dark hollows forming under his eyes. In his hand, he carries a bunch of flowers. He drags his eyes up to meet mine.

"It's over, baby."

∼

I run to him, flinging my arms around his neck. He presses his lips into my shoulder, and I shudder. I never thought I'd feel his warm, hard body against mine ever again.

"I'm sorry I locked you in," he says, dropping the flowers on the table. "It was an impulsive decision. I didn't trust you not to do something stupid."

"Thanks a lot," I say, punching him in the chest. There's more I could say about it, but I'm too relieved to see him. I look up at his face and see he's covered in blood.

"Jesus, Leo. What did you do?"

"I made a mess," he shrugs, "but that happens sometimes. The important thing is that the bastard is dead, and Pavel has asked the *komissiya* to stand down the hit. I have to go home and face the music, but—"

He has more to say, but I don't care. I pull at his belt, dragging his body to me so I can mold myself to him. His hand winds through my hair as he lowers his face to mine. His lips are warm and gentle, and he teases me, kissing me lightly when he knows I want more.

"I'm not gonna lie to you, *tigritsa*," he says between kisses. "I was afraid today. For the first time, I doubted myself. I had to do it, and it was a massive fucking risk, but now it's done, I feel fantastic."

I break away from his lips and look at him, confused. "You've killed so many people, Leo. What was different this time?"

He laughs and runs his fingertip over my lower lip.

"That's not what I mean. Killing the senator was a cakewalk. Telling you I love you? That was fucking terrifying."

His cell phone beeps, and he takes it out to look at it.

"Can I keep your attention for just a minute?" I pout.

Leo pockets his phone. "You kept my attention for the last three years without even being part of my life. You're *everything*, Ali. Do you think I would put myself through all this and not be all in? You and Luna are my priority now."

He drops onto one knee and smiles at my dumbfounded expression.

"I haven't got a ring." He picks up the flowers and extracts a single rose, holding it out to me. "And these flowers are from an accident black spot. I couldn't find a florist open, and I just killed a guy, so..."

I laugh. I can't help it.

All my life, people talked in hallowed whispers about *Volk Smerti*. The Gurin Bratva's assassin, the man who never missed a kill. If you saw him, you were dead. I can't imagine it'd do his rep much good if anyone knew this side of him.

But *I* know who he is, or at least who he *could* be. His love for me warmed him inside and made him give up something more valuable than his life.

He just found his heart, and now he's entrusting it to me.

"Are you gonna ask me?" I say. "You're kneeling in front of me with the blood of my enemy smeared over your face and a flower meant for a dead person. When people ask me to tell the story of how you proposed to me, it's gonna be one to remember, that's for sure!"

Leo grins and takes my hand. "Ali. You crashed into my life three years ago and lodged yourself in my heart. I tried to get you to fuck off and leave me to the lonely life I knew, but you kept fucking with me. I never even *thought* of another woman. Then fate got sick of hinting and hurled you into my path again, giving me a chance to earn your trust and, maybe, your love."

He smiles as I catch a tear with the back of my hand, and he kisses my fingertips. "Marry me, and I'll spend every day proving myself worthy of you and Luna. And," he yanks my wrist to his mouth and bites it, "I promise to fuck you senseless whenever you want."

"Ow!" I yelp, pulling my hand away.

"What's it gonna be, *tigritsa*?" Leo gets to his feet. "Can you handle me?"

I narrow my eyes at him. "Oh, you fucking *bet* I can handle you. But I don't want to be in the Bratva. I told you - I want a clean life."

"So do I," he says, grabbing my waist and pulling me to him, "and I know the best thing for that. A shower."

"That's not what I—" My words are cut off by his lips on my neck.

"I'm gonna get naked, and so are you," he murmurs against my skin. "Is that clear?"

I nod, melting into his hold.

"That's my good girl."

18

Ali

Leo heads for the bathroom, pulling his shirt over his head as he goes. He doesn't need to say anything. I'm right behind him, wriggling out of my t-shirt and bra. He steps out of his remaining clothes and is gloriously naked, his cock thickening as he turns on the shower.

"I want to make love to you, Ali," he says, admiring me as I slip out of my leggings and panties, "but I'm not going to. There'll be time for that, but I have to burn off the stress right now. You gonna take what I wanna give you?"

Fuck, *yes*. I know what he means. He needs my body to relieve him, just like I need his. Fuck the fear and uncertainty into submission.

"I want it," I say, stepping into the water flow. "Hurt me good."

Leo grins as he joins me. "You're a quick study, Ali, but you didn't have much to learn from me."

His cock is hard as ever, thick and solid as it reaches for me. He strokes it as he takes in the sight of my body, my tits shiny as the water runs over them. I sink to my knees, my mouth level with his shiny tip.

"Open up and suck it," he commands. "I have plans for you, but you don't always play fair, and I'm getting off first this time."

I clamp my lips closed and shake my head. He looks down at me, his expression darkening.

"You bratty little slut," he growls. "I love it. Do you wanna fight over it? 'Cause you're gonna lose."

I bat my eyes and smile so he knows I'm down to play. My clit is already swelling, brushing against my pussy lips. Leo grins back at me and wraps my hair around his fingers; with his other hand, he takes hold of my throat.

I exhale slowly through my nose, thrilled at his strong fingers compressing my neck. I don't know when I started craving that sensation. Maybe it's like heroin - the first time is enough to get hooked. But every time, it gets to me more and more.

Leo's cock brushes my lips. I want to take him in my mouth, but I resist because I know he wants to *make* me do it.

He releases my hair and grips my nose, pinching my nostrils closed.

"Can't you breathe, baby?" he asks as I flinch. "Take a good deep breath, *tigritsa*. Open up wide, so I can shove my cock straight down your fucking slutty little—"

Unable to hold out any longer, I gasp and open my mouth. With a roar of triumph, Leo's hand moves from my nose to the back of my head, holding me in place while he fucks my throat. His cock hits my tonsils hard, making me gag, the thick saliva coating his shaft and making it easier for him to slide in and out.

"Oh yeah," he groans, pumping his hips as the warm water cascades over us. "Your mouth is mine, Ali. Your pussy, your ass - every part of you is gonna be filled with *me*, always."

I couldn't stop him if I tried. His grip on me is too firm, too insistent. He pulls free of my mouth, breathing harshly as he lets go of my neck and grabs his cock. He pulls my hair, yanking my head back so he can jerk off to the sight of my tender neck.

"It fucking turns me on to see where I marked you," he says, stroking the throbbing tip of his erection over the livid fingertip bruises. "I'm gonna come on your face. Keep it out of the water."

He grips his shaft harder, his fist a blur as he chases his climax. He cries out as he comes, his seed catching in my eyelashes as it runs down my face and over my lips.

Leo looks down at me, breathing heavily.

"Get up, baby. Let me see that face."

I move to stand, and he helps me to my feet. My knees and quads ache, but the warm water revives me. He puts his hand between my legs, parting my quivering pussy lips and massaging my clit. My legs threaten to buckle, and my arm shoots out, steadying me against the tile wall.

Leo chuckles. He reaches out and rubs his entire hand over my face, moving his come over my skin. He grips my chin and pulls at my jaw, parting my lips. I gasp as he licks my face from my jawline to my eyebrow, gathering his come on his tongue before plunging it into my mouth.

"Taste me," he murmurs as he kisses me. His lips are hot and slippery from the water and his come. My pussy responds to his touch, soaking his fingers as he works my sensitive clit.

"Turn around," he says. "Put your hands on the wall and touch your clit. I'm gonna hurt you, just like you asked."

I assume the position, mewling with need as he rubs his hands over my ass. I know he's gonna spank me, and I'm so ready for it—

Leo's hand crashes into my ass cheek, and I almost hit the ceiling. He grabs the scruff of my neck and shoves me face-first into the tile.

"I'm telling you to touch yourself, Ali," he says, hitting me again. I'm astonished to feel him growing hard again, his cock swelling in the crack of my ass as he presses against me. "Because I'm a nice guy, I'll give your tight little pussy something to squeeze while you come."

"You're not a nice guy," I gasp.

Leo laughs, lining up his erection with my twitching entrance. He slaps my ass again as he plunges into me, my cheek pressed to the wall as he fucks my pussy. I rub my clit frantically as he pounds me, his hand raining down blows on my skin, my nerves alight with sublime pain and unbearable pleasure.

Leo leans close to my ear, pulling my head back to meet him.

"You had enough? Do you want me to hurt you some more, or do you need to come?"

"I need to come!" I cry. "Keep fucking me!"

He needs no more encouragement. He releases my neck and grabs my ass cheeks with both hands, kneading the flesh as he picks up speed. As my orgasm seizes me, I put both hands on the wall and brace, letting him fuck me through it.

"You love it when I rail you, don't you?"

I can't respond. My sore throat only makes a rasping sound as I come down from the peak. Leo pulls free of me and drags me back to him, his cock still hard against me as the water takes the sting away from my ravaged body.

∽

We lie in the dark, listening to the rain. Leo is behind me, his limbs entwined with mine. He runs his hand along my inner arm, tracing my bracelet with his fingertip.

"Tell me what haunts you, Ali. You've been afraid for a long time, haven't you?"

I close my eyes, trying to remember without it getting hold of me. The memories hijack my limbic system and propel me back into the moment if I don't concentrate.

"I saw my parents murdered. I was only four." Already my voice is lighter, more childlike. Leo slips his hand into mine, and I grip it tightly, but he stays silent. "I was hiding under my bed. My mother was bleeding, and she fell to the ground. I saw her dead eyes staring at me. Papa begged for me to be spared, but..."

The words die on my lips, and I begin to shake. The room blurs.

Leo wraps his arms around me like before and holds me tight.

"You can get past it, *tigritsa*," he whispers. "You're strong. So fucking strong. Don't let fear win. You are a warrior, remember? So *fight* it."

His words cut through the rising panic. I open my mouth and heave a deep breath as I grip the duvet with my fist.

I squeeze my eyes shut and make myself see it.

He has a gun oh no Mama can't help me and Papa is crying he can't speak why isn't he helping me I don't want to die...

I realize I'm mumbling the words, tears streaming down my face.

My eyes snap open, and I'm back in the room.

"Well done, baby. You're okay. You didn't let it get to you, not this time."

My cheeks are wet. I know I'm still crying, but he's right. I got past it.

"The man who killed my parents shot me, too. I was in the hospital for a while before they took me to an orphanage. I didn't speak again until I was seven, but I would hide under the bed at night until I fell asleep. When I cried in my dreams, they beat me for it, so I ran away."

"It's incredible you survived," Leo says, kissing the back of my neck. "Not just being shot, but on the streets too."

"Just lucky, I guess."

"No," Leo's voice is firm. "You gotta get into a new mindset, Ali. You're here because you fought for yourself, and now you fight for Luna too. Why do you think I call you *tigritsa*? It means 'tiger,' specifically a ferocious female cat ready to shred anyone who threatens her cub."

"I'd die for Luna without a second's hesitation."

"I know." He shifts onto his back, his hand idly stroking my thigh. "You know what I think? You need to fucking kill someone *yourself*. Someone who deserves it. It's hard to feel like a victim ever again once you know you're capable of that."

"Maybe." I turn to face him, placing my hand on his neck. He looks into my eyes. "If you love me, Leo, I need you to promise me something."

He nods. "Anything."

"If it ever comes down to Luna or me - if you have to choose one of us - *always* choose her. Don't let your love for me cloud your judgment. Don't save my life at the expense of hers. My parents died believing I was dead too, and the thought of what they went through is like a thousand daggers in my heart. I could face anything if it meant my baby girl would be okay."

"I'll promise you that gladly because it won't happen," he says. His eyes flash as though he's chasing away a thought, but then he smiles and pulls my head to his chest. "We're safe now. *All* of us."

19

Leo

"But why can't I just go on my own and get her?" Ali asks.

Understandably, she's confused. I told her she's safe, but I'm not sure. I received a message from Paval yesterday, and it wasn't the news I wanted.

Ben has gone to ground. Suspect you are right and he has started something he can't finish. I will keep you updated.

I know Paval will have people combing our territories to find the traitorous prick, so he probably won't get far, but I'm tense while he's still out there.

Could I tell Ali what's up? Of course I could. But I'm still basking in the warmth of her trust. And love, although she hasn't said it. I dare to believe she *feels* it.

If I let her in on the whole sorry mess, she'll know that she's in danger because of me. And even if we somehow get past this, that's unlikely to change. Once she comes down from the high of escaping almost certain death, she'll understand that being the wife of a Pakhan is a million miles from the safe, peaceful existence she wants for herself and Luna.

I could *force* her to marry me, obviously. That would be the Bratva way of resolving the issue. But I love her, which means I couldn't look into her eyes every day, knowing that I coerced her into a life of misery.

I wonder who I've become. The writing was on the wall when she and I first met, but she's demolished all my defenses and trashed my beliefs in just a couple of days. But the me *I* know - the part Ali fears - is still in there. The part of me that wants to see Ben bleed for trying to hurt the woman I love.

"Ali, you're not going anywhere without me. It's not up for debate."

"So because I agreed to marry you, it's gonna be whatever you say, and you don't have to explain yourself?" She glares at me, but the fight goes out of her, and she slams herself onto the couch, picking up the television remote. She taps on her phone, not looking at me.

"Please just hurry," she says, her tone cold. "I need to see my girl."

∽

I take twenty-five minutes to comb the place, picking up stray hairs and wiping down the surfaces. Pavel will see to it that no one looks too closely, but I'm not willing to take unnecessary risks.

I'm packing up my weapons when I hear Ali exclaim in shock.

"Leo!" she cries. "You bastard! What the fuck did you do?"

I turn to look where she's pointing. The TV is playing the local news, a special bulletin. The newscaster looks flustered as she struggles to read from the teleprompter.

"We're returning now to our top story, the murder of Senator Adrian Coffey in his home yesterday evening. Concerns are growing for the safety of the senator's wife Moira and five-year-old son Eddie, who have not contacted police or their family since yesterday morning."

A reel of shaky nightcrawler camera footage. Coffey's house, the window shattered. A blurry still image of his feet sticking out behind a privacy screen, with little flags marking forensic evidence.

"What did you do to his family?" Ali cries. I whip around to look at her and see she's shaking with fury.

"I didn't do anything to them, Ali. I don't know what—"

"I'm so fucking stupid. Why did I trust you?" She drops her head into her hands. "I asked you not to kill innocent people, Leo. I told you what happened to me, to my parents, and you comforted me when all the while you knew you'd... what? Are they dead?"

I move toward her, but she leaps over the back of the couch, backing into the kitchenette. She grabs a knife from the block, brandishing it in an overarm grip.

I'm strangely proud of her. She could do severe damage if she threw her anger behind that arm.

We stare at one another for a few seconds.

"Drop the fucking knife," I say. "We don't have time for this bullshit. I thought you wanted to go get Luna?"

There's a buzz on the intercom, and we both jump. Ali doesn't take her eyes off me as she reaches for the handset on the wall beside the refrigerator.

"Hi, Rox," she says. "Come on up!" She leans on the button to open the door and replaces the handset.

"So you told her where we are?" I throw my hands in the air. "Ali, I thought you were smarter than this. I have to go to Pavel and sort this shit out, and I'm taking you and Luna with me. I didn't fucking kill the senator's family."

"You're still not telling me everything." Ali's eyes shimmer, but she won't let herself cry. "You know something important, something you're keeping from me after everything I shared with you."

The door to the apartment opens. Ali gives me a look of desperation, and I understand.

Don't let Luna see this.

Ali puts the knife down and pushes past me, sweeping our little girl into her arms.

"Mumma!" Luna cries. She gives me a shy wave over Ali's shoulder. "Hi," she whispers.

Ali glances at me. Her emotions are palpable - anger, fear, but also love. Just for Luna, or for me too, I can't tell.

"I'm so glad this shit is over," Roxy says, dumping Luna's bag on the floor. "The last couple of days have been batshit crazy."

Luna wriggles in Ali's arms. Ali puts Luna down, and Luna skips out onto the balcony, standing on her tiptoes so she can peep over the railing. Ali's eyes are soft as she looks at her for a moment before turning back to me.

"I'm not going anywhere with you," Ali says, lowering her voice so Luna doesn't overhear. "If there's no threat to Luna and me, then you did what you came to do. I don't want any part of whatever you're trying to pull. I could see a future for us in the heat of the moment, but I was wrong."

Roxy looks from Ali to me and back again before hurrying onto the balcony. I hear her talking to Luna.

"Ali, I meant everything I said. I want you to come home with me. Be my wife."

Her expression is cool and impassive, but I see her lip quiver.

"You're a bad influence. On my daughter, and on me." She looks away, unable to meet my eyes. "I want to get away from you. I feel too raw with you, too open. I want to shut it all down, and I can't do that and be around you."

She rolls her bracelet around her wrist, fiddling with the heart-shaped charm. I reach to take her hand, but she pulls it away.

What can I possibly say that wouldn't be bullshit? I know how she feels because I feel it too. I fell for her long ago, and it fucking *changed* me. If I could go back and prevent that from happening, maybe I would. How can I blame her for wanting to protect her heart?

"Don't do this," I say. "I know you're afraid, Ali. But you don't have to be. I'll stand by your side forever."

"I don't want you," she replies.

~

Ali

The words are a lie. But I can't take it anymore.

I love him.

It's too intense for me to live with. I never knew how much love could hurt. I've been afraid before - fear and I are old friends - but to fear the one you love is absolute fucking agony.

Maybe over time, I can convince myself this was all a bad dream.

I need him to go. To return to his life. But it sure as hell isn't what I *want*.

Leo knows my deepest pain. He held me as I regressed to the child I was when my world fell apart. I never thought I'd feel that kind of dependency again. But here I am, horrified to find myself needing him in every way possible.

I can't risk my heart. I keep it alive for Luna, but she takes all I have to give. Trust is too flimsy a concept for me to bet it all on this man. He claims to love me, but even now, he's lying to me.

"Look," Leo says, his tone hardening, "you and Luna are coming with me. I'm not leaving you here. I'm her parent too. There's a genuine possibility that this shit is not over at all, and—"

I slide my bracelet from my wrist and open the locket, holding the tiny frame close to Leo's face.

"You see this?" I say. "There are the only pictures I have of *my* mother and father. All I have left of the love and security I once knew. I want Luna to grow up safe, with a clean slate and at least one loving parent. Better than me, and certainly better than you. Is that so fucking hard to understand?"

Leo tilts his head to look at the two tiny photos.

"You look like your mother, Ali," he says softly.

I want to punch him and kiss him simultaneously. It's precisely this dichotomy that I can't live with.

Leo's eyes slide across to the other picture. He frowns, then snatches the bracelet from my hand.

"Give it back!" I say.

Leo ignores me, holding the pictures closer to his face so he can see them better.

"Holy shit," he says.

A shot rings out.

20

Ali

Leo grabs me, hurling me to the ground. I see Roxy fly backward into the room, smashing into the side of the couch.

She's not moving.

My vision swims as panic seizes me. I scramble like a woman possessed to where Luna stands on the balcony. Leo grabs my ankle, but I kick him in the face with my other foot, and with a grunt, he lets go. I reach Luna and pull her into my arms, feeling her little body shake.

Leo's nose is bloody from where I kicked him. He doesn't seem to have noticed. He reaches up to the countertop, grabs his handgun, and crawls in front of us.

"Move back as far as you can," he says. "Get to Roxy."

I shuffle backward on my ass, pulling Luna with me. Roxy is leaning against the couch, blood staining her jeans from a wound in her thigh.

Luna's bag is beside me. I reach inside and remove the cord from her little bathrobe. It only takes a couple of seconds to fashion it into a tourniquet around Roxy's leg, and she smiles weakly. Luna sits between us, pale with shock. I cuddle her close as I dial emergency services. I babble the address to the shocked dispatcher, and then I ring off. My daughter quivers on my knee but doesn't say a word.

Leo is perfectly still on the ground, and for a moment, I wonder if they shot him without me noticing. Then he stands up and walks out onto the balcony, firing as he goes.

Luna is too afraid to scream. I reach into the holdall and find her bunny, trying not to get blood on it. Her music player is tucked into the bag's side pocket, and I grab it, quickly putting the headphones over her ears. I hit play, barely noticing the tears streaming down my face.

~

Leo

Ali is crying. I can't hear Luna, and I'm losing my fucking mind because I'd rather she was screaming the place down than silent. But I can't turn around.

All I need to see is the slightest movement and—

That's it. I'm on my feet, firing round after round at the figure on the rooftop opposite. My handgun is a subcompact pistol and a fucking nightmare to fire accurately at this range, but my senses are heightened, and the third shot hits its target. The man drops out of sight.

I hear a commotion in the stairwell. Whoever Ben hired to come for us, they aren't exactly ninjas. I assume they wouldn't have taken the job if they'd known who they were taking on.

I snatch up the kitchen knife and throw open the door to the apartment, gun in the other hand. I know the magazine wasn't full, but I don't know how many rounds are left. *Gotta take it easy.*

A swift kick to the stairwell door sets it swinging, and I duck around the corner again, avoiding a smattering of gunfire. There's a lot of artillery power down there with very little expertise behind it, and those people are the fucking worst in situations like this.

A man is running up the stairs. I fling myself around the corner shoulder-first, sending him rolling down again. I'm about to shoot him when Ali appears behind me, bundling Luna into my arms and taking the knife from my hand.

"Take her!" She cries. "Go, Leo! Get her away!"

"I'm not leaving you here!"

She kisses me, her lips salty from her tears. Then she shoves me in the chest.

"Fucking *go*! I'll be right behind you!"

I hold Luna's head to my chest so she doesn't see, and shoot the guy on the ground. The three of us run down the stairs and burst through the door into the light.

Ben is there. He's in his car, revving the engine.

He grins at me and releases the brake. The car powers toward us.

Ali doesn't move as quickly as me. She's behind me and doesn't see what's happening until it's too late.

I drop my gun and grab Luna with both hands as I fling myself out of the car's path. As my body shifts, Ali sees the danger and stumbles back through the door into the porch. Ben slams on the brakes, but he can't slow down fast enough.

The car smashes into the building, the hood folding in like an accordion. I'm getting to my feet, my eyes scanning the wreckage.

I see Ali.

She's unhurt, but she's inside the building, trying to climb over the top of the car to get outside. The crumpled driver's door creaks open, and Ben falls out. He's injured, blood running from his head where he smacked it on the dash.

His gun is in his hand. He looks up at Ali and sneers at her.

I dropped my pistol near the apartment door. He could shoot me five times before I get to it. Luna's tiny hands clutch at me. My eyes meet Ali's, and she sees my dilemma.

She shakes her head.

Always choose her.

She made me promise never to risk Luna's life for hers. But I can't watch her die.

Luna looks up and sees her mother. Her cry gets Ben's attention, and he turns to us.

"Hey!" Ali cries. "Come and get *me*, you fucker."

She's a fucking badass. She doesn't know who he is or why he's trying to hurt her, but she's standing there, ready to take him on, armed with nothing but a butcher's knife and her white-hot rage. He almost killed her kid, and she's still prepared to fuck him up.

Sirens are sounding nearby, getting closer. Ben looks from me to Ali, confusion writ large on his face. Still trapped inside, Ali drops down and is out of sight. Ben furrows his brow and gives his head a shake before trying to follow her, climbing over the wreck.

I turn and run for my car. Luna clings to her bunny but doesn't resist as I bundle her into the footwell beneath the front passenger seat.

"It's okay, baby girl," I say. "I'm gonna fetch Mommy, I promise—"

Luna is struggling to breathe. Her lips are turning blue as she gasps, looking horribly like her mother when she has a panic attack. I look back to the apartment door, but there's no sign of Ali, and Ben has disappeared too.

No time. There's nothing I can do. I don't know where he went, but my little girl will suffocate in front of me unless I get her some help immediately. If I go in and rescue Ali, Luna might die out here alone.

I know Ali doesn't want me, but I don't care. The pain of not being with her and Luna is *nothing* compared to the thought of them dying. Not when I was so close to saving them.

And not when they have more to live for than they realize. When Pavel finds out what really happened here, he might commit murder with his own hands, and it's been *years* since he did that.

I never trouble God for anything. I sincerely doubt He and I will ever meet. When I finally pass away, it's the other guy I'll be hanging out with.

But right now, I'm begging Him.

Don't take Luna.

Don't take Ali.

Let my family live.

21

Ali

I can't believe I told him I didn't want him.

It was a lie, and look what happened. As soon as we were in danger again, I turned to him without hesitation, and he didn't back away.

Seconds earlier, I told him to get out of my life, and he still put his own on the line for our daughter and me.

I run back up the stairs to the apartment. I reach the balcony in time to see Leo driving away as an ambulance pulls into the lot.

He has my daughter. I just got my little girl back in my arms, and now she's gone, borne away by the man I can't help but love.

The man who, just two days ago, came back into my life so he could end it.

It's crazy that I love him. *Insane.* I watch his car disappear into the distance.

He won't hurt her. I know it.

A voice interrupts my thoughts.

"Ali."

I run to Roxy's side. She's ashen, her skin clammy. The bleeding has slowed to a trickle, but she's lost a lot. The carpet squishes under my knees as I kneel beside her.

"Is Luna okay?" she whispers. "What happened?"

I take her hand. It's slick with blood.

"Leo got her out. He killed the guy who shot you. There was another guy who tried to run us down with his car. I thought he was following me, but he's gone, probably because he heard sirens." I weave my fingers through hers, squeezing. "Come on, Rox. Grip my hand."

Roxy tries, but her grip is feeble. "Ali, I just want to sleep," she murmurs, her eyelids heavy. "Just a couple of minutes. Then I'll be fine."

I shake her shoulder. "No way. Stay with me. I *can't* lose you, Rox. You've always been here for me."

Tears spring to Roxy's eyes, and she drags them open. I can tell she's struggling to focus. She looks slightly past me as she speaks.

"Don't let Luna grow up like us. Please. She deserves better. So do you."

"Fucking stop that," I say, my voice cracking. I scoop her head onto my chest, trying to keep her upright. "You're gonna be alright. *You* deserve a better life, too. Don't give up now."

"I'm so tired," Roxy says. "You have a future. You and Leo and Luna - you could be a family. A *proper* family. Wouldn't that be the *best* thing?"

I don't even know where they are. Now that I'm calming down, I'm thinking it through.

Why hasn't Leo come back?

Someone is running up the stairwell.

I suddenly remember the fire exit at the back of the building. If I'd thought of that sooner, I'd have escaped with Leo and Luna.

I scan my eyes over the room, catching sight of Leo's weapon stash. I snatch a pistol from the top of the pile and shove it down the back of my jeans, beneath my shirt. I zip the bag shut and roll it under the bed just in time.

I stand up as the paramedics burst in. One immediately pushes an oxygen mask over Roxy's face as the other two make a visual assessment.

"Gunshot wound," says the woman, darting her eyes at me. She presses a pad of gauze against Roxy's injury. "Anything else?"

"No, I don't think—"

They nudge me aside, carrying Roxy down the stairs. I follow, my entire body shaking. One paramedic jumps into the front of the ambulance while the other two carefully lift Roxy into the back.

"Are you coming?" The woman looks at me, raising her eyebrows. "The police will want to talk to you."

I hate myself for it, but I can't go with her. I shake my head.

The other paramedic secures Roxy on the gurney and turns to look at me, taking hold of the door handle.

"Some friend *you* are."

With that, the doors are closed, and the ambulance is away, lights flashing.

Instinctively, I reach for my wrist to stroke my locket's smooth surface.

It's gone. Leo took it from me not a moment before the shooting started.

I realize I don't have any idea what to do. Where to go.

The man who attacked us could be anywhere.

My breathing hitches. I clench my fists.

This apartment is soaked in blood and it's not safe here anyway and I don't know where Luna is where is Leo will he even fucking come back—

A thought cuts through my rising panic.

I can't stay here.

My phone is in my pocket, but when I take it out, it's smashed to shit. I don't know when it happened, but I suspect it was when Leo threw me to the ground.

My fear moves my feet. I gulp at the air as I go to the only place I can think of.

Leo

"Help her *now*!"

I carry Luna into the drugstore, trying to keep her upright. She's gasping, and every tortured breath is fucking terrifying me. The female clerk at the counter looks horrified.

"Sir, you need to take her to the ER—"

"There's no time," I say. I sit Luna on the counter, her tiny body convulsing as she leans on me. "Get me whatever the fuck will fix her. I swear I'll kill you if you stand there staring at me for a second longer."

The clerk disappears into the back, returning a few moments later with an inhaler. She shakes it and attaches it to a plastic mask, which she puts over Luna's mouth.

"Deep breaths if you can, honey."

Luna is losing strength. She's struggling to sit up, batting at the mask in her distress. I hold her arms, trying not to hurt her as the medicine takes effect.

"Come on, *milaya*," I say over and over.

Luna stills, then coughs. The clerk removes the mask. Luna slumps against me, but she's breathing. Quiet whimpers escape from her warm little body.

I scoop her into my arms again, handing her bunny back to her. She rubs its ear against her cheek.

I reach into my inside pocket and extract a money clip. I don't know how much is in it, but it's at least twenty thousand dollars.

I hand it to the clerk, watching her eyes widen with surprise/shock. "Give me a couple more of those, and keep the change."

By the time I get back to the car, medicine in hand, Luna is asleep. I lay her down in the footwell and drape my jacket over her.

～

When I arrive at the apartment block, the police are there.

Fuck. While I rarely worry about cops, I have no time to explain all this shit or get Pavel to deal with them. Especially not with Luna in the car. Ironic that I went around the apartment picking up every crumb, only for this shit to happen.

A tow truck is slowly dragging the crashed car away from the building. I leave Luna in the car, trying to act casual as I stroll over to the nearest officer. He's scribbling in his notebook.

"What the hell happened?"

"We don't know." The cop stops writing, glad of the distraction. "It looks like a dumb accident, but someone got shot on the roof over there, and inside, there's blood all over the floor."

Roxy. I guess the hospital and the feds didn't join the dots yet. That or she's fucking dead. Ali will never forgive me if—"

No. Tell me it's not Ali's blood up there.

"There are no bodies or anything?" I ask.

"No." The cop frowns at me. "Why? Should there be?"

I laugh. "You tell me, bud. You're the one to know. I watch too much true crime shit, that's all."

The cop isn't amused. "Okay, CSI Moscow," he says, "take your curiosity and dodgy accent elsewhere. I'm busy."

I sure as fuck have a lot to say to Pavel, but I'll tell him in person. Luna needs to be someplace safe, and when Pavel hears what I have to say, he'll move heaven and earth to protect her.

It's what Ali would want me to do. But I'll find her if I have to die trying.

∼

Ali

I'm home.

My apartment feels like a tomb. Only a couple of days have passed since I was last here, but when I crack open the door, the air inside shifts. It's as though all the people who lived here are now long gone.

And for all I know, they are.

I set the gun down on the kitchen counter and stare at it. I've never felt so alone.

I have no phone to call the hospital. Is Roxy alive or dead? I don't know. And there's no sign of Leo and Luna.

I can't hold my thoughts down. They lash at my brain, stoking the fears I've been trying to suppress.

Maybe Leo just wanted Luna. It would have been better for him to have me around too - as he said, he'd have to get married anyway, and Luna needs looking after - but he's not going to risk coming back for me now. He has an heir, a way to consolidate his position.

My stomach plummets as though I've just gone over the big drop on a rollercoaster.

Could it be that he knew all along? Is *he* the real reason that I was targeted? I thought he was protecting us because he loves me, but I know he was lying to me about *something* right from the start. I turned away and tried not to see the things that scared me.

Because I wanted to *love* him more than I wanted to *hate* him. And now I may have lost Luna forever.

I don't know where to look for her. If I go to the police, what the fuck will I tell them? No one ever took down *Volk Smerti*. What would be different now? He's *Bratva*. The cops aren't exactly friends of mine and are probably all on Pavel Gurin's books, anyway.

I told Leo to get out of my life, and he has. But I never meant for him to take our daughter away with him.

I go into Luna's room, and it's colder than ever. Her little quilt is crumpled in a ball where she left it on the night Leo came to us.

Luna is my reason to live. There are a thousand things I could do. *Should* do. But all the strength that was building inside me - all the things *he* gave me - it's all fading away.

I lie on her bed and pull her quilt to my face, breathing her in. The tears fall, and they feel hot on my chilled skin.

I dig my fingernails into my palms as I clench my fists. My sorrow churns into a boiling, agonizing rage.

All he has to do is bring her back. But if he walks through that door without her, I swear I'll fucking kill him.

22

Leo

"Pavel!"

My shout rings through the house, but there's no response.

I'm half-dead with panic. If someone already got to *him*, I'm fucked.

I don't think Ben is dead. I don't think Ali is dead, either. There's no way to know for sure. But I have to find her.

As things stand, I've gone rogue. Refused to complete a hit, murdered the client, and disobeyed the Pakhan. All Ben *appears* to have done is carry out Pavel's orders, and there's no one but me to say otherwise. My stock is far too low for my version of events to be believed, and *I* killed all the witnesses to this mess.

"Where the fuck are you, Pavel?" I cry.

Luna furrows her little brow at me. "Y'okay?" she asks.

I press my forehead to hers, relieved to hear her speak. "Yeah, baby girl. Don't worry."

To my surprise, some big guy I've never seen before is coming down the stairs, pistol in hand.

"Back up, *Volk Smerti*."

"Get that gun away from me," I say, glaring at him. "I'm holding my child. What the fuck is wrong with you?"

The man ignores me. He points the weapon at me and pats me down with his other hand.

"He's clean, Boss," he calls over his shoulder.

"Leo!"

Pavel is hurrying down the stairs. He looks astonished to see me.

"Holy fucking shit," he says, looking at Luna. "This is your daughter! There's no mistaking her. Look at her eyes!"

"What the hell is this?" I say, gesturing at the goon.

"I got some guys to protect the house. Until I know what's happening, I'm taking no chances."

He leads me into his lounge. I look out the window and see several more men patrolling the grounds. Luna coos, and I set her down so she can play with the soapstone chess set on the table.

Pavel pours me a drink and hands it to me.

"So what do *you* think is happening?" he asks.

I look at the family photo on the wall as I reach into my pocket, pulling out Ali's bracelet.

Pavel's breath catches.

"I never thought I'd see *that* again," he murmurs.

"Ali and Luna aren't just *my* family," I say. "They're *yours* too." I flip the locket open and hold it up. "These are pictures of Ali's parents. I recognized Bogdan." I search Pavel's face, looking for a reaction. "Somehow, your niece is alive."

There's a long silence. Pavel watches Luna as she shuffles the chess pieces around on the rug.

"I know."

"You know?" I'm on my feet. "Then why the fuck did you let this happen? You could have stopped all this. Why didn't—"

My words tail away to nothing as I see the man in the doorway. His instincts are sound, and instead of aiming at me, he points his gun at Luna.

Pavel is laughing. I haven't seen him this amused in a while.

"Sit the fuck down," he says. "*Now*, Leo. I'm not playing around."

I sit in the armchair and lean foward, my elbows on my knees. "I'm sitting. Now tell your lackey to stop pointing his gun at my child."

Pavels ignores me. He tilts his head as he gazes at the photo on the wall.

"I fucking *hated* him." He turns to me. "Bogdan. That fucker almost ruined my life. And *you* had to fall for *his* daughter -

the daughter I fucking shot in the head. It's as though you brought the bastard back to life."

No wonder I couldn't make it fit together. The senator was right - Ali *is* the key. But it's not because of *me*. It's because of her connection to *Pavel*.

"So you knew Ali was your niece?"

"Let's go back a bit here." Pavel sips his drink. "My father knocked up his side piece, and when she was jailed, he took the child into our family. Everyone *knows* that part. But Papa *loved* Bogdan's mother. My Mama tried to accept it, but she couldn't take it anymore and took the easy way out."

Holy fuck. That's why Pavel's mother killed herself?

"Papa couldn't look at me after that. Every time he saw me, he saw his dead wife, and the guilt ate him up. He put all his energy into Bogdan, but I threatened the cunt, told him to back off. He started pulling away from us. After he got married, he stopped speaking to my father and me. Broke Papa's heart."

I look at Luna, who is quietly humming as she arranges the pawns in a neat line.

I brought her here. My daughter is in the one place I thought she'd be safe, but now Pavel is telling me that his life is a lie.

"Papa always hoped Bogdan would come back into the fold, but I wasn't prepared to accept the possibility. So I staged a lovely little scene. Made it look like Bogdan had murdered his family and hanged himself. My father refused to mourn him and never spoke his name again. Every year, I enjoy the memorial, and all my associates come to comfort me for the loss of my beloved brother in such tragic circumstances."

"Pavel," I say, reaching for Luna. "I don't need to know all this. I can—"

"Leave the girl where she is, handsome," says the goon, clicking off the safety on his gun. "I can take her head off from here, no problem."

The words are out before I can stop myself.

"Hurt my daughter, and I'll beat you to death with my bare hands."

Pavel laughs. "You bought into your legend, didn't you? You're just a *man*, Leo. As you know, men die easily. Pathetic that a woman and her child brought you down, but appropriate." He knocks back his drink. "It's bad enough that the little bitch somehow turned up alive, but for my most loyal soldier - my *chosen heir* - to fall in love with her and give her a child? You fucking *idiot*. You had it all. I was willing to give it to you, and this is how you repay me?"

I can't focus on anything except the threat to Luna. I need Pavel to get where he's going with this so I can do whatever's necessary to get the fucker at the door to lower his weapon.

"How did you find Ali?"

"I didn't *find* her," Pavel spits. "If she weren't a thieving scumbag, I'd never have known she was still alive. I had the senator's data stick stolen, but when Coffey came to me complaining about it, I watched the security footage. I recognized Ali, and that fucking bracelet confirmed it beyond doubt. It belonged to Bogdan's wife, Starla, Ali's mom. And before that, Bogdan's whore mother."

I look at the bracelet for a moment. The woman in the picture has Ali's stormy eyes and fine bone structure.

"I got the senator on board easily," Pavel continues. "He knew what I'd done to Bogdan - he was the chief of police at the time and helped me cover it up. I told him it was me who had his data stick stolen, and I would give it back in return for him approaching the *komissiya* and requesting a hit on the girl who stole it."

Pavel stares at the picture as though he wants to reach into it and strangle his brother all over again.

He seems to enjoy unburdening himself and letting me know how clever he is. Like all narcissists, the urge to showcase his own genius is too much to resist. If I act like I doubt his methods, he might keep talking.

"That seems a fucking risky strategy," I say.

"Does it?" Pavel sneers. "*I* think it was fate that Ben's guy hired Ali for the job. Once I had the senator under my thumb, all I had to do was wait for you to complete the hit. It shouldn't have been risky at all. You've killed hundreds of times and never missed the mark. But no, you had to come at me with this wildcard shit. I've been chasing my tail ever since, but you proved incredibly easy to manipulate. Tell me - how many people are alive now who can bear witness to this?"

"No one except this fucker," I nod at the man with the gun, "you, me, Ali, and Ben. I killed everyone else."

"Ben knew nothing except what everyone else will soon know - that you, *Volk Smerti*, killed a government official without authorization, then tried to take me down too." He grins. "Where is Ben? Did he get Ali? Don't tell me you left the poor bitch to fend for herself!"

I *did* leave her. And if he's still out there, he might be looking for her right now. She might be dead already.

I've had enough of this shit. He's enjoying himself, and I can't look at his fucking smug face anymore.

"What do you want?" I ask.

"I want you to go back, and fucking kill her yourself. Like you were supposed to."

"I'd ask if you're insane," I say, "but I already know the answer. Fuck yourself, Pavel. Why don't you just kill me?"

"I worked far too hard to get to this point!"

Pavel turns suddenly and slams his hand on the table, making Luna jump. She looks from him to me, her lip quivering.

"Coffey tried to back down when he found out you were refusing to kill the girl, and the people involved were dropping like flies. Even the threat of being exposed as a child molester wasn't enough, and he said he would tell the *komissiya* everything. Do you know what would happen to me if they found out what I did to my brother and his family?"

Yes, I do. You'll be torn to pieces for it. They do not tolerate the murder of family members in cold blood.

He killed them. That's what the senator said to me. I thought we were talking about Ben, when the whole time, *he* was talking about Pavel.

Luna is crying, trying to clamber into my lap. I put her on my knee and hold her close, my hand on her cheek. The gunman opens his mouth, but Pavel holds up his hand, silencing him.

"So you kidnapped the senator's wife and kid as an incentive for him to keep his mouth shut?" I ask.

"Yep." Pavel grins. "But in the end, it was easier just to let you kill the fucker. You were right. He *was* a liability." He waves a hand at me. "Don't worry; they're perfectly safe, you know. In custody."

"Ali thinks *I* murdered them."

"Leo, Leo." Pavel shakes his head sadly. "So will everyone else. What is the point in carrying on? You're no good to her. She's dead no matter what. You should have killed her at the start and spared her all this shit. I told you, but you didn't listen."

It's coming together in my mind.

Fate didn't bring Ali to *me*. It brought her to *Pavel*. When he saw her in those security stills, he wanted her dead and found a way to make it happen without him being connected to it. I let him down, and he tried to hide his involvement and make Ben the fall guy hoping Ali and Luna would be killed before I could figure it out.

But I kept them and myself alive. Until now, when I walked into the lion's den with my innocent daughter and no gun.

Pavel took me in and treated me like a son. I never guessed the depths of his bitterness. He was a distant but benign presence in my life, but it never entered my head that he could do something like this, least of all to me.

I never knew him at all.

"Is it worth it?" I ask. "Ali doesn't know she's related to you. She can't remember what happened to her parents. I could give Luna back, leave them alone, and pretend none of this happened."

"No. She could remember any time and fuck me up." He walks around the table and sits on the chair nearest to me, reaching out to Luna, but I turn away, shielding her. He scowls, but doesn't push it – instead, he takes a step back and fixes me with a glare.

"I'll tell you what's gonna happen here," he says. "You're gonna go back and find Ali. If she's dead, bring her back here, and if she's alive, kill her first and *then* bring her back here. This little one will stay here with me as insurance."

Zoya comes in and gently extracts Luna from my arms. I'm about to tell her to go fuck herself until I realize I'll frighten my little girl.

Luna is calm and goes without a fight. It burns me to let her go, but I can see I'm out of choices, and I don't want her to think anything is wrong.

Zoya sees me pain and sneaks me a look of sympathy. "I'll look after her," she says.

"Her asthma medicine is in my glove box."

I pick up Luna's bunny and hand it to her as Zoya turns to leave.

Luna waves at me over Zoya's shoulder, and I smile. She's so innocent, so trusting. Her world has been a safe place up to now, and she's too young to take in what's been happening over the last few days. My heart skips a beat as she vanishes from sight.

I turn back to Pavel, unable to keep the venom from my voice.

"Why the fuck would I agree to this?"

"I thought the world of you, Leo," Pavel says, patting my shoulder, "so I'll make you a deal. Kill Ali, and I'll let you take the kid away from here as long as you never return. Ben can take your place. *Won't* kill her? Then I'll get hold of her and have the pair of them trafficked. Some of Senator Coffey's friends would be keen to meet the little cutie."

Bile rises in my throat.

"You fucking sick—"

"Don't bother," Pavel says. "The last thing Bogdan heard was me promising to kill his little girl. I *will* see it done. And just bear in mind that I am being very fucking generous given all the trouble you've caused me."

He looks at his wristwatch. "You'd better hurry - if Ben is still looking for Ali, you might have to fight over her corpse. However you do it, you'd better come back with her body by tomorrow morning, or your daughter will be famous on the Dark Web."

23

One hour later...

Ali

I can't look at Mama. Something is happening to her face - every time I glance at her, she changes into me, then back again.

What am I holding? I look down to see a toy bunny in my hands —Luna's bunny.

But Luna isn't here. It's me, Ali, with my dead Mama and dying Papa.

His voice is choked as he struggles. Mama's blood creeps toward me.

. . .

I feel my consciousness clawing at the edges of the scene. Normally I'd fight to get out of this nightmare, but I want to stay this time.

I never saw Luna here before. Never felt her. It's as though she's leading me deeper.

Don't fight, Ali. Let yourself drown in it. Let it swarm over you. *Feel* it all this time.

I look out from under the bed and see my father standing on a chair. There's a thin piece of wire around his neck, secured to the beam in the ceiling.

A man stands beside the chair with his back to me. He's nudging Papa's feet.

"You fucking cunt," the man snarls. "Your bitch mother seduced my father. Broke my Mama's heart. She'd still be alive if it weren't for him. If it weren't for you."

My father's mouth opens and closes, his feet slipping.

"Anything to say?" the man asks. "I thought not. Well, it's all over now. I'm not letting you have what's mine just because our father loves you more. I was here first, and I'll be here last. You're not my brother. Never were. I'll tell everyone you did this to your family."

Papa gives a strangled cry of anguish as the man laughs at him.

"Devil," Papa says. The wire is tight around his neck. "No."

Devil.

Davil.

Pavel.

Pavel.

Pavel.

Pavel Pavel Pavel PavelPavelPavelPavel—"

"Pavel," my father gasps. "Don't hurt my daughter, please!"

"She's dead, Bogdan. Die knowing it."

The chair clatters to the ground and he grabs my ankle and pulls me into the light and there's the gun oh God no—

I sit bolt-upright in the recliner, heaving air into my lungs.

When did I move? I don't even remember getting out of Luna's bed. The gun is no longer on the counter; instead, it's beside me on the arm of the chair.

I'm losing my mind.

My father was named Bogdan. Half-brother to Pavel, Pakhan of the Gurin Bratva.

Pavel Gurin is my uncle. He killed my father.

I don't know what to believe anymore.

If Leo took my child to that man, I'll—

Someone is trying to open my apartment door. It's locked, but that doesn't deter the intruder. A muffled shot blows out the mechanism, and I hear the hinges squealing as the door is pushed open.

∽

Fifteen hours later...

Leo

The sun is up on the day of Bogdan's memorial.

The man who killed him will make a massive fucking deal out of how much he misses him and his family.

It's sick. But it'll soon be over.

There aren't as many guards as before, but I guess Pavel doesn't need them anymore. It's considered very poor form to use an occasion like this to cause trouble, so he isn't anticipating issues with his guests.

The barrel of Ben's gun digs into my spine as he walks me across the lawn toward the house, nodding at the handful of men outside. One of them even opens the door for us, and I recognize him as the bastard who threatened Luna. I can only imagine how satisfying it must be to see *Volk Smerti* on the end of a gun. The idiot can see I'm at an obvious disadvantage but insists on making a show of patting me down. I don't even have a knife, let alone a fucking gun.

Ben jostles me into the lounge.

Pavel looks well-rested. He took Ben's call an hour ago, and now he's sitting here with his breakfast tray like it's just an average morning. I look around and notice several large floral arrangements waiting to be placed in the sunroom. He went for the lilies in the end.

Ben shoves me into the same armchair I sat in the previous evening and presses his pistol to my temple.

"So this is fucking hilarious," Pavel grins. "Loverboy here goes to find his woman, only to walk straight into her apartment and find you *and* her dead body?" He looks at me. "You had a really shit evening, didn't you?"

"Just let me leave with Luna," I say. "Wasn't that the deal? You won, Pavel. You're gonna get away with it."

"You aren't going anywhere until I see her. I want to look at her face and know I've finally kept the promise I made to my brother." He puts his palm on his chest. "I'm a man of my word, you know."

Pavel goes to the door and waves two men over.

"Go to the car and bring the body in here. Put it on the floor."

It's only a minute before they're back, carrying the body bag with them. They don't show any respect, dumping it on the rug in the center of the room. Pavel looks at the photo on the wall as he points at the body.

"Look at that, Bogdan!" he cries. "A full house! You're back together as a family. Isn't that nice? Your little girl can rot beside you."

Ben laughs.

"You let people believe your brother killed his wife and daughter?" I ask. "That's low. Pavel. And you lied to the *komissiya* for years."

Pavel wheels around and looks at me. "You think I should be *ashamed*?" he snaps. "I've never regretted killing them. His wife and child were innocent, but so was my mother, and she fucking died, so I don't see how it's any different."

"Bogdan was innocent too. And after all these years, you find out that his daughter is alive and go after her? She never did a thing to you."

"I don't care."

Pavel walks over to the body bag and bends down, unzipping it roughly to reveal Ali's face. Her lips are purplish, her skin white. He stands and leans over her.

"You wanna see how much respect I have for your whore?"

He hocks in the back of his throat and spits on Ali's face.

I can't stop myself. I'm halfway to my feet when Ben slams a hand onto my shoulder, pushing the gun harder into my head.

"Don't fucking try it," he hisses.

"Yeah, you're a veritable genius," Pavel laughs. "Trying to defend the honor of a dead slut when your daughter is alive and kicking? I've got news for you, Leo. Your kid isn't going anywhere with you except a hole in the ground. Did you really think I'd let you walk away from this after everything you put me through?"

I tried to play along with him. Even after everything I've learned, I wanted to believe that there was *some* decency in him. But I was wrong.

I hear Luna in the distance somewhere, singing a song.

Please don't come in here, baby girl. I don't want you to see your Mama like this.

Fifteen hours earlier...

Ali

I slide to the ground, taking the gun with me, and roll out of view behind the couch. The curtains are closed, and it's fairly dark in the room but not dark enough to hide for long.

I check the magazine. There are only three bullets. *Shit.* I'm a decent shot, but one in three isn't great odds. I risk peering around the edge of the couch, and I see a figure standing there, gun in hand.

He takes two steps toward me, and I know. I can tell by the way he moves.

Leo is back. And this time, he's gonna kill me for sure.

I duck out of his eye-line and drop my head against the couch, fighting the tears.

The father of my child has stolen her away, and now he's back to tidy up the loose ends. There's only one explanation that makes sense.

Pavel is the one who wanted me dead, and now that it's all come out, Leo has agreed to fulfill his original contract and kill me, presumably in exchange for his own life. Who can blame him? I told him I didn't want to be with him, so he has little to gain by letting me live. Why would he lose everything for *me*?

I have to find out what has happened to our child. I can't die not knowing. He's faster than me, but I might be able to hold him off long enough to get the truth.

I draw a deep breath and roll out from behind the sofa, gun in hand. As expected, Leo ducks back around the corner as I appear.

"Ali, what the fuck?" he shouts. "Put that down."

"You're the one who's creeping around my apartment with a gun!" I scream. "Where is Luna? You're *so* full of shit. You know Pavel Gurin is my uncle, don't you?"

"I *do* know that, but—"

I shoot, the bullet blowing a chunk of plaster out of the corner. My ears are ringing, and I can't hear Leo's words, but after a few seconds, I can make them out.

"I didn't know until today. I saw the picture of your father in your locket and recognized him. I took Luna to Pavel because—"

"You took her to him?" I cry. "He killed my parents!"

I'm already flagging, my resolve leaving me fast. My gun feels unbearably heavy all of a sudden. "He put the hit out on me, didn't he? The murdering piece of shit sent *you* to tidy up after him. Takes one to know one, right?"

My head is spinning.

My parents were murdered by Leo's boss, the man to whom he owes *his* life. So now Leo is finally gonna kill me, and I'll never know what happened to Luna...

I'm overwhelmed with sorrow and collapse onto my side, barely holding on to the gun. Leo breaks cover and runs to me, dropping his weapon as he sinks to his knees.

"Don't touch me!" I sob, trying to focus as I lift the gun. "Leave me alone or kill me. I don't fucking care! I thought you were *saving* Luna, but you took her away, and now I'm gonna die feeling nothing but terror for my child, just like my own parents!"

Leo lies down facing me. He grabs the barrel of my gun and rests it on his forehead.

"You want to kill me, *tigritsa*. God knows I understand." His ocean eyes look past the gun, trying to hold my gaze. "With your gun in my face like this, I'm powerless, so take your time. Do it if you must, but *choose* it."

I'm shaking, but Leo remains motionless. He never takes his eyes off mine.

"You're incredible," he whispers. "A warrior. Remember when I said that? I meant it then, and I mean it now."

I can't shoot him. There's no way. Even now, his voice reaches into me, a balm to my raging emotions.

"Easy, Ali. Get a hold of yourself." He reaches out and rests his hand on my hip. "There's a lot you don't know. I was lying to you, but not in the way you think."

I close my eyes and move the gun away from Leo's head. He takes it from me and clicks on the safety before tossing it aside.

We look at each other for a long, painful moment.

"What happened?" I ask.

∼

The explanation takes a while. By the time Leo lays it all out for me, the sun is long gone.

"It's fucking horrible, but simple," Leo says. He's sitting on the couch, his gun beside him, as I sit on the floor like a kindergartener. "Pavel sent me back to kill you. As punishment for my transgressions."

"You could have just run."

Leo throws me a glance. "You think I'd leave you to fend for yourself? Never. I told you - the possibility of me dying is not a concern to me unless it will lead to you and Luna coming to harm. Pavel led Ben to believe that I'm trying to launch some kind of coup, so he must think it's funny to turn me loose too and see what happens next."

"That seems kinda crazy. What if you went back with a bunch of armed men?"

Leo smiles at my naïveté. "He knows I don't have anyone to call on. I'm *Volk Smerti*. Almost everyone in our world has cried over the coffin of someone I blew away. As Pakhan, that would have inspired fear and respect, but as an outlaw, it just means that no one is gonna take up arms for me." He cocks his head as though something just occurred to him. "I have *one* friend," he says, "Kal Antonov. We trained together with the *Spetsnaz*. I haven't spoken to him in years. But his father-in-law is the new chair of the *komissiya*, so I can't ask him to get involved."

"I still think Pavel is insane," I say. I pull my hands into my sleeves, trying to warm them.

"Maybe the old bastard *is* finally losing his marbles. But whatever is going on, he has Luna. He expects me to bring you to him cold tomorrow morning, so he can have this wrapped up before Bogdan's memorial wake. The *komissiya* members will come and pay their respects, as usual."

"What would Pavel tell them? Surely they'd want an explanation for what happened to you."

"He'd just make something up. He knows I'd keep his secret. I could never risk Luna's safety just to bring that bastard to book for what he's done. If the *komissiya* found out what Pavel did, they'd remove him and give me the Bratva. But I'd have to prove it, and Pavel has Ben to back him up."

I feel sick to my stomach. The thought of my child being held captive by my parents' killer is more than I can take.

"Do you think he'll keep his word? I'm so scared, Leo. What if he hurts her?"

"I don't think he'll do anything tonight. His housekeeper is looking after her, and he's got guests tomorrow. If I don't show up, he will get rid of Luna before any of them arrive."

"Why did he hate my father?" I ask. "All he did was exist. He didn't ask to be born. It seems like a lot of trouble to kill me too, just because my Papa loved me."

Leo sighs. "Pavel is a warped, bitter old man. He's delegated so much to his underbosses that he has too much time on his hands, and this is what happens when old wounds are left to fester. I wanted to keep his legacy and look after his empire for him, but now I don't give a fuck what happens to it. I just don't want a war to break out over the scraps."

His head lolls against the couch. After the day we've had, it's not surprising that he's ready to drop. I lean against his legs, resting my eyes.

"You're gonna have to kill me, Leo," I whisper. "There's no other way."

"I can't," he says. "You'd have to do it yourself. But that's not on the cards either."

"What *are* we gonna do?" I murmur.

"I'll think of something," he replies. "But one thing's for sure. I'll see that old fucker dead for this."

24

Four hours later…

Leo

I open my eyes to see Ben.

Fuck knows when he came into Ali's apartment. I must have heard him through my haze of sleep, but I remember nothing before the moment I snapped to consciousness, my gun already in my hand.

He has his pistol trained on Ali. She's quivering on the floor beside me. "Ben," I say. "Let's not do anything rash, okay?"

The gash in his head is no longer bleeding freely, but it needs suturing, and one eye is swollen shut. I doubt he could have seen well enough to shoot any of us back in the parking lot, but he sure as hell could hit Ali just fine from this range.

"She looks like someone," he says, squinting at Ali. He's slurring his words, and I wonder if he's concussed.

"She's Pavel's niece, Ben. He duped you and me both. "

"The fuck you say?" Ben shakes his head as though he has a fly in his ear. "Bogdan's kid? How?"

"I'm going for my pocket. Sit down and point the gun at me — *Ben!*" I shout to get his attention. His eyes are glazing over, and I'm worried he'll accidentally squeeze the trigger. "Point the gun at *me*, not Ali. *I'm* the one who could shoot you."

I can tell his heart isn't in it. That or he's about to keel over. I reach into my pants pocket and retrieve Ali's bracelet, handing it to him.

"Open the locket and tell me who you see."

He looks at the pictures, then at Ali.

"Jesus," he says.

"Wrong. It's actually Bogdan and Starla. Ali's parents. Pavel killed them. He told me so himself."

Ali nods. "It's true."

Ben frowns. Then he laughs.

"He told me you'd gone rogue and betrayed him. That he wanted you and Ali dead, and as long as I didn't ask questions, the Bratva would be mine. He assured me your kid wasn't with you, or I'd never have agreed to it."

"Did you think *you* could take *me* out?" I ask, unable to keep the doubt out of my voice.

"On my own? Fuck no. That's why I hired two guys and ambushed you. But you're too fucking good at what you do, aren't you?"

I don't even credit that with a response.

"You hurt yourself when you crashed the car?" I say.

"Sure did." Ben taps his temple with the barrel of his gun. "Real crack to the nut. When I saw you had your daughter, I couldn't bring myself to go after you, and I had no appetite to take out Ali, either. So I went to the safehouse and slept it off for a while. When I called Pavel, he told me he had your child. He said I had to kill you both by tomorrow or not bother coming back."

I frown at him. "You're not having any trouble believing what I say. Why?"

"Because you *love* them." Ben puts his gun on the floor. "I could convince myself of anything until I saw you defending them, Leo. You had to turn your back on Ali because of me, and I saw your face. You fucking *broke*. I knew Pavel had to be wrong. After all, you loved *him* too."

"So you didn't come here to kill me?" Ali asks.

Ben cocks his head and smiles at her. "Not this time. I thought Pavel might pull some shit, but he's gone way off at the deep end with this. I *was* looking for you, but only to help."

I search his face, looking for the lie, but I can't see it. All this time, I thought he was pulling the strings, but he had nothing to do with it.

"Shoot me if you want, Leo," Ben says, raising his hands. "I thought I wanted the Bratva, but I was in over my head. I nearly killed your family, and there's nothing I can do to atone for that."

Ali is on her feet.

"If you *could* help," she says, her stare boring into Ben, "would you?"

Where is she going with this?

"Anything. But there's nothing left. Pavel has your daughter. You die, or she dies, but not before he makes her suffer."

Ali's eyes are aflame with fury, but she's smiling. She turns to me.

"He wants me dead? No fucking problem."

***

Five hours later...

Ali

I'm so cold. If I could feel anything other than anger, I'd be in agony, but every nerve is seared with a numbing, vicious rage.

I am going to murder this piece of shit.

All my life, I was afraid. The child in me never found closure, and I never knew how much I yearned for the love I lost. I was too broken to grieve, too raw to accept what happened. As much as I tried, I couldn't push the pain deep enough.

Leo brought it all rushing to the surface. He bound me to him by setting me free, and this is the final stage. The last nail in the coffin before I really can bury the past.

I feel heavy footsteps shaking the floor, and hear the rasp of the body bag's zipper. I close my eyes and hold my breath, trying to relax my muscles.

I'm glad I can't look at Pavel. I need to choose my moment; seeing him might override my reasoning. But where he was muffled before, now I can hear him loud and clear.

"You wanna see how much regard I have for your whore?"

A wet coughing sound.

He's gonna spit on me. Don't move, don't react—

His saliva is wet and disgusting as it hits my face. Despite my efforts, I cringe, but he must have turned away and not seen it.

Leo is stalling, keeping the bastard talking. He's saying plenty. Why are people like Pavel always so keen on the sound of their own voices?

He's talking about my Mama and Papa.

They never meant to leave me. Pavel Gurin stole them and their love away, and for the longest time, I wished he'd killed me too.

But not anymore.

I open my eyes a sliver. Through my lashes, I can see that Pavel has his back to me. Leo is sitting down, Ben's gun to his head.

I hope Ben is on the level, or we're fucked. He's laughing at the shitty things Pavel says. Either its subterfuge, or Leo was an idiot to trust him, but they've been friends a long time—

Luna.

I can hear my little girl singing. It takes everything I have not to jump to my feet and run to her.

"Pavel," Leo says, his voice cracking, "please. Ask Zoya to take Luna away."

"Thought you'd want to see her." Pavel steps into the hallway and yells. "Zoya! Take the kid back upstairs while I deal with this."

"This is a bad thing you're doing, Mr. Pavel," Zoya replies. "She's just a little girl. It's very wrong for you to—"

"Fuck off!" Pavel snarls. "I don't answer to you, the *komissiya*, God, or any other fucker. Get out of my sight."

There's a strain of hysteria in Pavel's voice. It's as though he's grasping the enormity of what he's done - what he's *doing*. But he's too far gone. The wheels have come off for him, and he can't see a way to stop.

"Don't kill my daughter," Leo says as Pavel walks back into the room. "It's unnecessary. She's a baby. She won't remember any of this. Give her up to a hospital or something. Let her have a chance."

"Like Ali?" I close my eyes again as Pavel turns to gesture at me. "The roads weren't paved with gold for *her*. Now the pretty thing is dead, *you're* about to be dead, and as for Luna…I haven't decided. Maybe I'll traffic her anyway, make a dime or two that I don't even need."

I'm supposed to wait. Listen out for cars arriving, and let Leo and Ben spin this out for as long as possible. But my fury is boiling over.

This man killed my parents. He tried to kill me *twice*. Threatened my child with torture and death.

For the first time since I was four years old, I'm not channeling my emotions into fear.

I push Roxy's voice recorder into the pocket of my jeans, hoping it's done its job. I might have taped over her lectures but something tells me she'd forgive me.

My hands slide to my hips, pulling the pistols from the twin holsters.

I'm reaching out to grab vengeance by the blade. I don't care if it cuts me.

I sit up, throwing the body bag off my shoulders.

Leo's eyes widen.

"Not yet, Ali!"

"Surprise, Uncle Pavel!"

I unload a round from each gun into Pavel's chest, sending him spinning into the wall. Blood spatters across the large framed family photo above him.

25

Leo

Everything happens at once.

Ben pulls the gun from my temple and wheels around to the open window, shooting the guard outside before he even realizes there's anything wrong. As the dead man crumples to the ground, Ben spins to the doorway, neatly removing the kneecap of another guy coming to see the commotion. He screams as he goes down, falling behind the couch.

Ali throws a pistol at me, and I snatch it out of the air.

"Get to Luna!" she says. "Ben and I will cover you."

I don't want to turn my back on her again, but there's no other option.

I run into the hallway and up the stairs. The front door opens, but I don't turn around, and I hear rapid gunfire as the guard peppers the lounge with bullets.

Don't be hurt, Ali. You took Pavel down. All you have to do is survive the next couple of minutes.

I kick open three doors before I find Zoya and Luna in a small bedroom. Zoya made it as comfortable as possible, with a soft quilt on the bed and a television on the wall. Luna sits on the floor, eating something from a bowl.

"Crispies," she says, holding up her spoon. She looks past me onto the landing and frowns. "Noisy."

"I know, baby," I say, light-headed with relief to see she's alright. I turn to Zoya.

"You've been at Pavel's side for years. Did you know about this? What he did to his family?"

"No," she says. "But he's a terrible person. Not the man you thought you knew. He's done evil things to me too, Leo. I never dared to believe I'd ever be free of him."

I hate myself for not noticing Zoya's pain. The hundreds of times she's brought me drinks, served food and taken my coat. I never knew she was a slave because I never truly *saw* her. I never paid attention to anyone except Ali and Luna.

There's no time for this now.

"Keep Luna here," I say. "How many men are patrolling?"

"I think there were six."

I can't hear any gunfire downstairs now, and no one has followed me. I don't know whether that's good or bad.

Then I hear Ali.

"Luna! Leo!"

"We're up here, baby," I yell. "How many guys are down?"

"We took out four," she says. "Ben is down but not out. Why? Are there—"

Her voice cuts off, and I run onto the landing to see two men at the bottom of the stairs. Ali is halfway up, frozen to the spot. Both men have their weapons trained on her.

"Drop it," one of them says. "You're so fucked now."

A crunching sound from outside, accompanied by the rumbling growl of a large engine.

Pavel's guests are arriving.

∽

"What. The. Fuck."

Fyodor Pushkin isn't impressed with the scene before him. I have to concede that it looks pretty bad.

Four dead men. The fugitive *Volk Smerti*, gun drawn, his woman armed and blood-spattered on the stairs. And that's before he sees what happened to Pavel.

A familiar face appears in the doorway behind Pushkin. A face I haven't seen for many years, not since I first got back from *Spetsnaz*.

"The fuck you doing, Leo?" Kal asks.

"Of *course* you know him," Fyodor says, glaring at Kal reproachfully. "Why am I not surprised?"

For a long moment, no one says anything. Fyodor moves to stand in front of a guard.

"You know who I am?" he asks.

The man nods nervously.

"Good." Fyodor taps the barrel of the gun with his fingertip. "Then you'd better get this out of my face immediately, hadn't you?" He turns to address everyone. "Put your fucking weapons on the ground, or I'll kill you all myself."

Lots of clicks as we all make our guns safe and put them down. Kal reaches into his jacket, pulling out a handgun of his own.

Fyodor frowns. "You aren't supposed to bring that here. It's a memorial wake," he looks at the bodies in the hallway, "or it was fucking *meant* to be. What happened here?"

"Leo called me this morning and warned me something was gonna go down," Kal says, nodding at me. "Why do you think I insisted on coming? I don't even *know* Pavel Gurin, and it's way too fucking early in the morning, but my brother-in-arms gave me a heads-up."

"You're welcome, *tovarishch*," I say.

"Oh no," Fyodor barks. "Don't fucking start with the *Spetsnaz* fraternity thing. We're not sucking each other's dicks. I want to know what the fuck you're playing at, *Volk Smerti*, and I want to know *now*."

The bedroom door opens a crack, and Zoya peers out. She raises her eyebrows at me, and I nod.

Luna runs unsteadily onto the landing and sees her Mama.

~

Ali

I try to go to my baby, but my legs give way. I drop to my knees and crawl to the top of the stairs, snatching Luna into my arms and squeezing her tight.

"My sweet girl," I say, kissing her over and over again. "I thought I'd never see you again. Are you okay?"

She puts her little hands on my cheeks and smiles the gappy grin I adore.

"M'okay, Mumma. Y'okay?"

"Sure." I let the tears go as I hold her to me. "I'm fine now. Sorry I was away so long."

The housekeeper is standing in the bedroom doorway, looking at us. She smiles.

"Thank you, Zoya," I say.

I pick Luna up, cradling her to my chest. Leo moves towards us and wraps his arm around my shoulders.

"A lot happened here, Fyodor," he says to the man downstairs. "Can we go into the lounge and discuss it? I promise it's worth your time to listen."

Fyodor looks like he'd rather kill him. He glances at Kal, who shrugs.

"If you hadn't listened to *me* in a similar situation, I'd be dead," Kal says. "These fuckers aren't gonna be able to walk away from what they've done. Aren't you interested in *why* they did it?"

It's an awkward moment as we congregate in the hallway. We step over the dead guards, and Leo pushes the lounge door open. I hold Luna's head to my shoulder and turn my body away so she can't see.

Ben is pale. He's been shot in the shoulder, but he's got pressure on it, and I think he'll be alright. He's lying on the couch as though we caught him napping, and tries to sit up when he sees us.

"Stay put," Fyodor says to him. "We'll get to you."

Pavel is slumped against the wall, still breathing. His chest wounds suck with each breath, a sure sign of at least one punctured lung. The pool of blood beneath him spreads ever wider.

"Leo is crazy," he spits, his voice a grotesque rasp. "His woman too. They attacked me in my home. An innocent man who did them no harm." He looks at the two guards. "Come on, you fuckers. Speak up!"

Everyone looks at the men who were trying to kill us only minutes ago. There's an uncomfortable silence.

"I just work here," one of them says, looking sheepish. "I don't wanna be involved with this. You had a kid hidden away…"

Fyodor looks at Pavel, then at me. He cocks his head.

"I swear we've met. Who *are* you?" he asks.

"I'm Alina Gurin," I reply, "but I didn't know that until yesterday. He killed my parents, Bogdan and Starla. He thought he killed me too, but he failed."

"She's insane," Pavel whines. "They both are. I treated that boy like a son, and he turned on me. Betrayed me."

I take the voice recorder from my pocket and hold it up for Pavel to see.

"Do you know what this is?" I ask. "You were so desperate for Leo to understand you, that you never stopped to think whether you should be running your mouth."

Pavel glares at me, his expression souring as he catches on. He knows he can't deny it now.

With that, the last pieces of the facade crumble away, and he lets his true ugliness show.

"You little bitch. Your father deserved it. I was a kid who needed my mother, and he took her from me!"

He's crying, but only for himself. It's a pathetic sight. He's like a mirror of me - a child who lost his parent, twisted up in grief and misplaced rage. But where I turned in on myself, he lashed out.

"So this is true?" Fyodor says. He walks over to Pavel, kneeling to his level. "I knew Bogdan and Starla. And I knew the young Ali." He turns back to me. "I can see it now. You look like them both, but your mother more so. Do you remember me, *dorogoy*?"

I shake my head sadly. "I wish I did. God knows I'd give anything to feel close to them."

Pavel laughs and spits blood at Fyodor. It hits him on the chin, and he wipes it away with his tie.

"Boo fuckin' hoo," Pavel sneers. "Doesn't change a thing. They're still dead."

Fyodor sighs. He nods at Kal, glancing at me.

"I think we should let her have this one." He raises his eyebrows at me. "What say you, Ali? You wanna end him? Strictly speaking, I shouldn't do this, but who gives a fuck? You've been through enough."

Kal holds out the pistol to me. I look at it for a moment, but there was never any doubt. I hand Luna to Leo.

"Take her outside. Let her look at the flowers. I'm gonna finish this."

Leo kisses the top of Luna's head, then leans to me, brushing his lips over mine.

"You're incredible, *tigritsa*. I'll see you in a minute." He closes the door behind him.

∼

He pulls me by the ankle into the light he has a gun I want my Mama where is Papa is he hurt is he dead I don't want to die too I'm so scared why why why why why—

The cold metal in my hand stills the panic of that little child who never thought she'd know a life without nightmares.

I have the gun now.

Peace floods my nervous system like heroin, soothing my tortured nerves.

I'll sleep soundly from now on. Never again will I dream of the terror I felt when this man took everything from me.

I can't bring my parents back. But I'm still here. Despite the odds, despite the many ways I should have died by now, I've made it.

We made it. Leo, Luna, and I will go on living. *Together.*

Pavel tries to raise his hands and cover his face, but he hasn't got the strength. Good. I want him to look at my face and *feel* the fear, just like my Papa had to. Like *I* had to.

I rest the barrel of the pistol against Pavel's forehead, feeling his skin shift over his skull as I press.

"I'm alive, Pavel," I say. "Die knowing it."

I squeeze the trigger, and it's over.

26

Two hours later…

Ali

Roxy is in the hospital. It took Fyodor Pushkin less than five minutes to locate her, and thirty minutes after that we were at her bedside.

After we called ahead, she was moved to a private room. Ben is next door, sleeping off his stitches.

Despite blood loss and severe shock, Roxy is okay. The bullet hit her femur but somehow avoided the artery, so they removed the slug from her leg and patched her back up before giving her a blood transfusion. The doctor says she's stable and just needs to rest and recover from her ordeal. Now she's dozing, coming around from the anesthesia.

Luna is sitting on my knee, eating a cheese sandwich that Leo got for her from the vending machine. I still can't believe she's safely in my arms.

Not five minutes after I shot Pavel Gurin dead, it seemed like every important Bratva member was there. Every family on the East Coast was represented, befitting the somber occasion. But they showed up for my father, not Pavel, so it took a lot of explaining to bring them up to speed.

Ben knew where to find the information we needed. Pavel had sense enough to have a safe, but it was no match for my well-practised fingers, and cracking it open was a cinch. Inside was the dossier Ben compiled on me, along with the senator's filthy little home movie, on the very same data stick that I lifted only a couple of weeks ago. It feels like a lifetime has passed since then.

You'd think, after everything, that I'd want to say my piece. But I was completely wrung out. It was as though all the pain I'd felt for years drained out of me, and I felt strangely weak. Still do. I'll have to learn to run on hope and love, instead of fear and grief.

Leo did a lot of talking, and once we got a stiff drink in him, Ben got his version of events across too. The *komissiya* members were shocked, but more than anything, they were angry. Angry that a man they trusted - a Pakhan, no less - had lied to them for so long.

Moira and Eddie Coffey showed up unharmed less than an hour after Fyodor put the word out that they were to be released. We turned on the television and left rolling news running until we saw the special bulletin confirming it. Because they were taken hostage under Pavel's orders, no one is gonna be punished for it—they're safe, that's the end of the matter.

We're going back to Pavel's house tonight. The *komissiya* have pooled their resources to clean up the mess so we can put the whole business behind us. Zoya said she'll stay, and I'm grateful. Thanks to her, my child is chattering away to herself now, her usual cheerful self. The events of the last couple of days seem to have slid right by her. Time will tell if that's true, but I don't want her to be like I was as a small child, and it looks like she may come through unscathed.

More than can be said for Leo and me.

Roxy is stirring. I touch her hand, and she opens one eye.

"Ground control to Major Tom," I say. She slides her eyes to me, trying to focus.

"I'm dead, aren't I?"

"Nope." I smile. "You're gonna be fine. We're all gonna be just fine, Rox."

Luna tries to climb on the bed.

"Woxeee!"

"Steady on, kiddo," she says, sitting up and wincing as she feels the pain in her thigh. "You can't climb on me. But if you'll sit nicely at the end of the bed, we'll put the television on for you, okay?"

Roxy nudges the remote toward me, and I find the cartoon channel. Luna lies on her stomach, dropping cheese on the bed sheet as she watches the show.

Roxy smiles at me.

"What happened?"

"So much, babe. I shot a bunch of people."

Leo pipes up from the armchair in the corner. "She *killed* a bunch of people. It was amazing."

She closes her eyes again, squeezing them shut as the pain grips her again. "You're a terrible influence, Leo."

"I know," he says, "but I'm so proud of her."

Roxy smiles at his words. She reaches for me and I slip my hand into hers. She rubs the back of it with her thumb.

"That fucking gorgeous man is in love with you," she murmurs. "You know that, don't you?"

"Yep."

"Are you finally safe?"

"We are," I sigh. It feels so good to be able to say that.

"So why are you here with me?" She fights her eyes open long enough to give me a mischievous wink. "Go be together. I'll be out of here soon. You guys need each other. Won't it be great to not be in danger?"

I ponder for a moment. Am I ever safe with a guy like Leo? I look over my shoulder in time to catch a flash of something in his eyes. Something that's gonna hurt in the best ways.

I turn back to Roxy, leaning in to kiss her cheek.

"You're right. See you soon, babe. Rest up."

"You too," she whispers as she nods off. "You deserve it."

When we get back to Pavel's house, it's like it never happened.

As promised, the place is clean. The lounge is sealed up for now, but the hallway is spotless, and everyone has gone, respecting our need for peace. There are things that need to be done, but all of it can wait. Zoya has made up a room for us, and she's making food for later.

The *komissiya* members brought flowers to lay on the memorial stone outside. After I put Luna in bed for her nap, we go out to take a look at it. The tributes are all laid out along the edge of the garden like a river of blossom.

It's a polished slab, built into the garden wall. The inscription simply reads:

A dearly loved husband and father.

It doesn't have his name. No mention of 'brother', or even 'son', and no stone meant for my mother or me. It strikes me that here, on my father's memorial stone, Pavel didn't bother to lie.

I turn to look at the old house, with its wide windows and bright green door.

"I want to live here," I say. Leo stares at me.

"Why? I know it's a beautiful house but it was Pavel's."

"It wasn't *just* Pavel's." I touch the stone, running my fingers over the letters. "It's coming back to me now. I remember this place. Before my Papa left the family, we used to come here and spend time with my Grandpa."

Leo takes my hand, pulling me to him. He kisses my forehead.

"If you feel close to them here, *tigritsa*, then this is where we'll stay. You're the deceased's next of kin, so technically you inherit it anyway."

We walk inside, and I take a deep breath. The metallic tang of blood has gone, and even the strong sting of carbolic has faded. I catch the scent that prods at my memory — old books and furniture polish.

I *remember*.

I used to skip up those same steps. Slide along the tiled hallway floor in my socks. Hazy, distant snippets of a time before Pavel Gurin ripped it all away. But my Mama and Papa walked these floors and occupied this space. The air reverberates with their presence. With their love.

Ours, too.

"Leo?"

"Yes, my Ali?" He strokes my cheek with his fingertip.

"I love you. I really do."

He kisses me deeply, cupping my face as his other hand steals around my waist.

"I know, baby. But I love you *more*, and that's how it should be."

My tongue finds his, and I'm hit with a sudden, desperate need to feel his skin on mine.

"For the love of everything holy, take me to bed."

I feel him smile. "What about for the love of everything *un*holy? Because that's how *I* do it, *tigritsa*."

～

The bedroom door closes behind us, and we fall on one another, pulling off our clothes. The tension, the terror, the rage — it's all melting together, becoming greater than the sum of its parts.

I need relief. I need him to ravage me until the fire inside has burned up all the debris I spent my whole life carrying on my shoulders.

Leo drags my jeans down my legs, taking my panties with them. He lunges for me, giving a growl as he sinks his teeth into my inner thigh. I gasp with pain as the skin breaks, slapping his face as he pulls away.

He sits back on his heels and I get a good look at him. He's naked, his skin seeming almost iridescent in the sunlight. He has my blood smeared over his chin, his eyes wild with desire.

I'm awestruck. He fucking terrifies me, but I want him so much I could die. My pussy floods as he licks his lips, tasting me.

"You hit me," he says, his voice thick. "That was hot as fuck. I really want you to do it again."

I'm panting already. He looks like he's ready to fuck me through the wall. I pull my shirt over my head, shake out my hair, and clamber onto my knees. We're face to face, tasting each other's breath.

"What do you want, Ali?" Leo says. "I'll give you anything. Because I'm in awe of you. Fear tried to rule you and you fucking *owned* it. You came up with a desperate, crazy plan," he draws a fingertip along my breast, flicking my nipple, "and got your vengeance at the end of a gun."

"I did." I shudder as he lowers his tongue to my rosy peak. "And you let me do it. Why?"

"Because I've killed hundreds of people and they meant nothing to me." He tweaks my nipple with his fingers as he kisses my neck. "You only needed to kill one guy to feel everything you needed to feel. Tell me, *tigritsa*. Are you still a victim?"

I sigh as his lips heat my skin. "No. I took my power back. Because you were right. I *did* need to kill someone who deserved it."

"Be honest." Leo bites my neck, sending a bolt of sensation to my core. "It felt good, didn't it? Like, really fucking good."

"Yes," I whisper. He groans in my ear.

"Oh fuck *me*, Ali. I'm so turned on to know you killed and loved it."

"Don't get used to it," I say. "I don't plan on making a habit of it."

Leo's mouth is supple and warm on my neck. Then without warning, he grabs my hair and pulls my head to one side, sucking at my skin like a vampire. I feel his teeth digging into my throat — not enough to make me bleed, but hard enough to bruise.

It hurts. *Fuck*, it hurts. But it's *so* good. My clit throbs as it swells, and my first instinct is to touch it, but instead, I pull my hand behind me and swing for Leo's face, delivering a ringing slap.

He doesn't hesitate. He releases my neck, keeping a firm hold of my hair, and slaps me back, whipping my head aside. Before I can catch my breath, he grips my chin and drags my face back to his.

"You beautiful, beautiful slut," he says, kissing me tenderly. The contrast between the kiss and what went before is obscene, but I can't deny the thrill it gives me. "You haven't lost it, have you? It's still in there. The part of you that wants to fight me, to hurt me. Say it."

I'm no longer afraid. He burns with passion for me, and I for him. I could never get enough of this man, the man I love, who fought to the death time and again to keep me and our child alive. I can lean into this and trust him now because he saved me, in every way a person can be saved.

"I wanna fight you, baby," I say, baring my teeth at him, "but not as much as I wanna fuck you. So bring it."

Leo's hand shoots out and grips my throat. His thumb presses into the tender spot where he bit me, and I sigh as the pressure relieves the throbbing pain. His other hand is between my legs, his fingers pushing into me.

"Dripping," he says. He brings his fingers to his mouth, licking my juice from them. "You're wetter than ever, *tigritsa*. Here."

I open my mouth and he reaches to the back of my throat. It's an incredible feeling to have his hand on my neck while I gag on his thick fingers. I choke up some of the thicker saliva that coats my windpipe, and he withdraws from my throat, rubbing my spit all over my lips.

"Get that mouth good and wet," he says. He reaches for his cock, using my saliva to lubricate his length as he pumps it. "How hard can you take it in your throat? Because I wanna pound it raw."

His breathing is ragged as he works his cock. Part of me wants to keep him here, hanging on, staring into my eyes while he jerks himself off. But I need him to direct that energy my way.

"I can handle you. Do it to me."

He pulls me down to the bed, pressing my face into the duvet. He removes his hand from my neck and grabs me, flipping my body so I'm looking up at him. I stick out my tongue, and he smears my saliva all over my face with the smooth tip of his cock.

Then he's on his feet, pulling me toward him. For a moment I think I'm going to fall off the bed, but he holds my shoulders, arranging me so my head is hanging off the bed upside down. I feel dizzy as gravity sends the blood rushing.

Leo's cock looms before me, looking even bigger from this angle. It's shiny with my spit, the head purplish. He grasps it at the base, rubbing it over my lips.

"Open up and relax," he murmurs. "I won't be gentle, and you're not gonna get a second to breathe, let alone speak."

I lap at the bead of wetness forming at the very tip of him, then clamp my mouth shut.

"You wanna play it that way?" Leo says, slapping my cheek with his shaft. "Fine."

He moves faster than I've ever seen him move before. I feel it before I see it – a stinging slap to my pussy. The shock forces my mouth open, but before I can cry out, he's inside, his hardness crowding my mouth. He holds my neck with one hand, the other poised to spank my sex again.

"Sass me again and I'll thrash your pretty little pussy until it's too sore for me to fuck it. Is that what you want?"

I can't reply. He's pumping his hips, scraping against my teeth. The corners of my lips are painfully stretched, my mouth struggling to accommodate him as he pumps in and out.

I bite down just a little. It's not enough to cause pain but I'm making my point well enough.

"I warned you. Keep it down and remember – you brought this on yourself."

Leo whips his fingertips over my pussy, and despite the pain, I open my legs wide, ready to take the next one right on my throbbing clit. He notices and laughs, shoving his cock deep into my throat as he leans over my prone body to get a better look. He lets go of my neck and reaches for my pussy, parting the puffy lips to reveal my deep pink hole.

I'm pinned in place, his cock deeper in my throat than I would have thought possible. I relax, giving my gag reflex a chance to calm.

He spits on my pussy and slaps it again. I seize up, my throat closing around his shaft, and he growls with satisfaction.

"Let's do that again," he says.

He holds my pussy lips apart and slaps my clit again and again. I leap with shock every time, my core aflame with sensation. My body has no idea how to respond. Pain, pleasure – it's all one. An engulfing, agonizing mess of sheer *feeling*.

Leo's cock bumps my tonsils with every nudge of his hips. How he hasn't come yet, I don't know, but one of us has to get there soon or we'll pass out from the intensity.

He pulls his cock free of my mouth with a growl, pushing me back onto the bed. I'm gasping, trying to sit up, but he has no intention of letting me. I'm just getting to my knees when he stands and puts his hands on me, flipping me onto my back. He grips my thighs and pulls them apart as he lowers his weight onto me.

"I wanna look at you when you come," he says.

His cock nudges my sore pussy, and just like when he grips my neck, the pressure soothes the pain. He shifts, trying to slide into me, and I take the opportunity to hit him again. It's a real bitch slap this time, the air splitting with a crack as it lands.

The effect on Leo is instant and extreme. His hand envelops my neck again, holding me to the mattress, and he roars as he plunges inside me, filling me deeply and completely in a single thrust. He stifles my cry with his mouth, crushing his lips to mine.

"I love you," he says between kisses, "because you were made for me. I'm so fucking–" he pulls out and shoves back inside me, making my breath catch, " –lucky."

He sits back on his knees, grabbing my ass so he can pull me closer as he fucks me. His free hand wanders over my breast, and he pinches my nipple hard.

"Can you come quietly?" he asks. He slows his movements, teasing my entrance.

I fix my eyes on his. "Give me something to bite?"

Leo no longer has the Band-Aid on his index finger, and the little wound is almost healed. He moves until the same finger is on my lips, the others still on my neck.

"I want you to decorate me with scars, *tigritsa*." His fingertip parts my lips, resting between my teeth. "All I want is to be covered in your marks. Tattoo me with your ecstasy, baby. Make me fucking bleed for you."

He slams into me again, his thumb pressing on my clit, and I can't help but close my teeth around his finger. He moans, hissing through his teeth as the skin breaks, his blood warm on my tongue.

"Oh *fuck* yeah," he says. I feel his cock thickening inside me, and I know he's close. "You gonna come for me, Ali?"

"Keep doing that," I say, "and I will."

"Such a good girl."

He finds another gear, railing my pussy as he swipes his thumb over my clit. He snatches his finger from my mouth and pulls his hand away from my neck, so he can wipe his blood on my tits.

The look on his face is enough to hurl me over the edge, and I throw my arm over my face, screaming into it as my orgasm crashes through my body. My pussy squirts lewdly around Leo's pumping cock, clutching wildly, and he comes deep inside, twitching as he empties his load into me.

∽

Leo

Finally, I can sleep.

Restfully, dreamlessly. The nightmares have receded, and my fondest dream is by my side. I no longer have to sleep to find her.

I stir to the sound of Luna chattering to herself. Ali rolls over, and I touch her shoulder.

"Stay there, baby. I'll get her."

When I go into the room, Luna is sitting up in bed, her bunny in her arms. Her new music player is on the nightstand, and on the floor is her big bunny. I pick it up and tuck it up beside her in bed.

"Does bunny need a nap now?" I ask.

"Yep." She looks at her tummy and frowns. "Is dinner?"

"If you want dinner, you get dinner, *milaya*."

She grins and reaches for me. She pokes me in the chest as I pick her up.

"Who you?" she asks, her little brow furrowing. It's as though she knows and trusts me but just remembered that she hasn't got a word for me.

I smile. "I'm your daddy."

Luna's mouth drops open. She puts her palms on my cheeks.

"Wow!" she cries. "Crispies?"

I can't help but laugh.

She's a stunning child. Her eyes are the same as mine, and her hair and bone structure are like Ali's. It's hardly surprising that of all the many questions asked today, no one questioned Luna's lineage for a second. If she was only beautiful, I could cope, but every word she says pulls at my heart. We're gonna have a lot of fun together but I get the feeling I'm in big trouble here – I'm already putty in her hands.

Zoya is in the kitchen. Something is cooking in the oven, a warm savory smell wafting through the house. Luna waves as we walk into the room.

"Hiya, lady," she says.

Zoya looks up, smiling at Luna and me. She has something laid out on the counter, and she's trying to scrub away the blood, worrying at it with a rag.

I take a closer look and see it's the photo from the lounge wall. The one of Bogdan and his family.

The picture Pavel secretly gloated over, secure in the knowledge he'd killed them all. Incredible to think that the four-year-old girl he left barely alive came back and destroyed him.

"I took it down before Mr. Pushkin closed up the lounge," she says. "You said Miss Ali has no pictures of her family except the tiny ones in her locket, so I'm trying to save this one for her."

"That's a good thing to do. Thank you."

An idea hits me. I set Luna on a stool at the counter.

"Don't worry about that for now, Zoya. Do you mind getting this bottomless pit something to eat? Whatever's cooking smells incredible, but I doubt she can wait."

"Crispies!" Luna shouts, clapping her hands. I shake my head.

"Nuh-uh, young lady. Real food. Something with vitamins. How about some fruit?"

Luna gives me the first of what I assume will be many eye-rolls.

"Daddy!" she grumbles.

Zoya chops apples while Luna chatters to her. I leave them to it, wandering into the hallway and out onto the porch. The afternoon is cold but clear, the sky a cloudless pale blue.

A week until Christmas.

I've never celebrated Christmas before. What do people do?

I realize it doesn't matter. I will do whatever the fuck Ali and Luna want. They have gone without for too long, and I'll make it my business to ensure that they want for nothing ever again.

First things first.

"Zoya," I say, sticking my head around the door, "you don't have to answer this now. But do you want to stay on indefinitely? As a real job, with a salary and all that shit. Luna likes you, and so does Ali." I smile awkwardly. "And for my part, I'm trying to, you know, be a real person. I can't take away the suffering you've experienced, but I can make amends as best I can."

A mischievous smile plays on Zoya's lips. "I'd love to stay," she says, placing a plate of sliced fruit in front of Luna. "I know a lot about this house that might interest you. Such as the lack of soundproofing."

I think about apologizing but decide against it. *Fuck it.* It's not my style to be ashamed of my basic nature.

I shrug, then smile at her. "Done. And if you could avoid commenting on the state of Ali's neck when she comes downstairs, that'd be much appreciated."

"Sure." She rummages in the drawer. "Do you want a Band-Aid for that finger?"

27

One week later…

Leo

"Leo!" Ali calls up the stairs. "The Pushkin-Antonovs are here!"

I laugh to myself. A very merry Bratva Christmas to one and all.

Roxy and Ben dropped by separately earlier in the day, bearing gifts. I still think there's something going on between them – they got friendly when they were in adjacent rooms in the hospital. Roxy is enjoying her freedom in the new apartment I got for her, and Ben is cagey about the subject, so if they are up to anything, I wouldn't know. I'll get Ali to work on Roxy and get the news, but not today.

I stop on the landing. The view from the top of the stairs is interesting, to put it mildly. Fyodor Pushkin is swearing as he tries to get through the door with a massive canvas sack. Ali is laughing at him.

"You could help," he grumbles.

Ali takes the bag of gifts and takes it through to the lounge, followed by the rest of our guests. I head down the stairs and stop in the doorway, admiring the room again.

There's no denying it — Ali did a fantastic job. She picked out everything from wallpaper to drawer handles, and just last week, we finished it off with a thick gold carpet and a beautiful cream marble fireplace.

The space above the mantelpiece is conspicuously empty. She's been talking about putting a mirror there, but it didn't happen, and I'm glad of it.

The Christmas tree that Ali, Luna, and Roxy picked out is in the corner. It's eight feet tall, flocked with fake snow, and garnished with red berries and pine cones. The branches groan with every decoration imaginable, from gingerbread men to candy canes.

I'll always cherish the memory of that shopping trip. The three girls were almost hysterical, delighted at the festive wonders to be seen. When I said they could have anything they wanted, Ali cried, and it still took several attempts before she understood that I was serious. Once she did, though, that was it — the three of them went to town. The place looks like a fucking grotto, and I don't wanna think of the electricity bill, but what the hell. I can afford it.

Recent events have rocked the Russian mob to its core. Family vendettas, coups, and betrayals are an accepted part of our world, but the cold, pragmatic murder of innocent people? That shit is *not*. The whole disgusting affair has reminded us all to appreciate the people we love.

With no formally nominated heir, the *komissiya* will oversee the dissolution of Pavel's empire. There'll be nothing left of the bastard. Everything he built will vanish, but contrary to how it usually goes, it will be sold off piecemeal in an orderly, civilized fashion. As his only living family member, the money goes to Ali.

That's not just the rules. It's also ironic. Pavel Gurin's death has set up his niece for life. She'll be richer than me, and although she didn't have to kill hundreds of people to get the money, she's still fought harder for her wealth than I ever did.

I glance at Fyodor and spot the spots of pink on his cheeks. His wife Marta catches my eye.

"He's half cut already," she says. "Did you know it's Kal and Dani's anniversary today?"

Ali looks at Dani. "Aw, that's so cute! You got married on Christmas Eve?"

"Sure did," Dani says. "Have you guys set a date yet?"

"We're gonna elope in the summer," I say. "Take Roxy and Luna with us. Make it a bit of a holiday." I clap my hands to get everyone's attention. "I'm gonna be a good host and get the drinks in. Any requests, or are you gonna trust me?"

Kal sniggers. "I don't trust you with shit, Leo."

Dani looks at him as she tries to wrangle their four-year-old daughter into sitting down. Tiana Antonov is very much her father's daughter; she's wriggling toward the tree, trying to examine the presents.

"I don't trust *you*, Kal," Dani laughs. "I thought you were joking about your *Spetsnaz* skills!" She turns to me. "You two can stay here and catch up. Ali and I will get the drinks so we won't start on shots."

Kal rolls his eyes. "All right. But make sure the vodka is cold because *Ded Moroz* over there," he tilts his head in Fyodor's direction, "is not sufficiently full of Christmas spirit. I've yet to see him drunk, so I'm working on it."

∼

Ali

"Thanks for inviting us," Dani says, retrieving two bottles of vodka from the freezer. "It kinda sucks that both my sister and Kal's are abroad, but they wanted a holiday. They both struggle with family in their own ways."

I smile. "I can understand that. I find it hard sometimes, and so does Leo. We're still trying to navigate family life, but it gets easier every day. I could get used to this. Having money is wonderful when you're used to scratching around in the dirt for everything."

"I can't pretend to relate to that." Dani gathers shot glasses, putting them on a tray. "I'm a Bratva princess through and through, as you should have been. But you're not entirely comfortable, are you?"

No, I'm not.

Leo said he would pay for Roxy and me to take night classes. She's gonna finish her counseling qualification, and I'll take social care. But I'll never get a job after I qualify—one look at my rap sheet, and no one's gonna take my calls.

"Truthfully?" I ask. "I'm not comfortable, no. I'm trying to lay my past to rest, but some of my choices cannot be undone, and I have to live with the consequences."

Leo appears in the doorway.

"Ladies, we're getting dry in there," he says. He takes the tray from Dani, giving her a grin. His hand reaches to take one of the frosty vodka bottles from the counter, but instead, he pushes my hair behind my ear.

"Pretty earrings," he says. "Which amazing son of a bitch got you those?"

I reach behind me and pick up the bottle, pushing it into his hand.

"Get outta here," I scold, giving him a peck on the lips. He raises an eyebrow at me and turns away, leaving Dani and me in peace.

For a moment or two, neither of us says anything.

"Ali," Dani says, avoiding my eyes, "I don't know you that well, but we're kinda friends now, right?"

"Sure." I pick up the other vodka bottle.

"So in that spirit," she says, leaning closer and lowering her voice, "I gotta know. Leo fucks like a monster, doesn't he?"

We dissolve into helpless laughter. I pull down my roll-neck, revealing the livid bruise above my collarbone.

"Is that an answer?"

Dani claps her hand over her mouth.

"I knew it!" she exclaims. "What the hell do they teach them in the *Spetsnaz*?"

~

Our guests are leaving, stumbling unsteadily down the drive to the car. Kal and Fyodor are singing a dirty version of 'Jingle Bells' as Dani carries the sleeping Tiana.

"Shut up, you two!" she scolds. "Mama, tell them!"

Marta shrugs. "It's Christmas, Dani. I know you're the designated driver, but that doesn't mean you get to be a buzzkill."

Dani thinks for a moment, then laughs. "Fair enough." She nudges Kal. "At least sing in tune, baby."

"I can't, my love," he says, grabbing her hand and kissing it. "What I lack in ability, I make up for in enthusiasm."

"The creed of terrible lovers everywhere," Leo laughs. Kal looks over his shoulder at him.

"From what my wife told me, *you* are fucking certifiable, *tovarishch*."

"Shh!" Dani hisses. She mouths the word 'sorry' at me. I glance at Leo.

"And just what did you tell Dani, exactly?" he asks. The twinkle in his eye gives him away, and I smile, relieved he's not angry.

"She asked, and I answered honestly." I take his hand as we wave goodbye on the doorstep. "It's just girl talk."

We shut the door and go back through to sit in the lounge, getting warm by the fire. Luna went to bed a while ago, and the house is quiet. Even Zoya is asleep, having taken herself off to her room earlier after one eggnog too many.

Leo picks up a present from under the tree and puts it in front of me.

"I hope you like it," he says. "I thought you might want to open it now."

I fiddle with my bracelet nervously. Something in his eyes tells me that this gift is important. The wrapping paper tears easily, and as I peel it away, I see *myself*.

It's a painting. A painting of me as I am now, standing in between Mama and Papa. Luna is there in my arms, and we're all smiling.

My eyes fill with tears.

"It was fucking difficult to get this done," Leo says. "Luckily, Fyodor had some photos of your parents. I gave the artist a couple of you and Luna, and he managed to put you together in one image."

I look at him. "You're not in it."

He shakes his head. "It's for you and *your* blood, Ali. The blood you share and the blood you shed. You'll never have this in real life," he points at the painting, "but you can hold them in your heart and see them every day. They'd have been so proud of you."

I gently rest the painting on the carpet and crawl into Leo's arms. He holds me close, his fingertips massaging the back of my neck.

"Thank you," I whisper. "For all of it. I never dreamed I'd be able to give my child a better life. And I didn't think I'd have you for keeps."

"Well, I'm semi-retired, and I never thought that would happen either," he says, "so that's an unexpected bonus. But I have you, *tigritsa*, and I don't regret any of it. If we'd never met, I would have seen out my life, never knowing what I was missing."

I smile as I wipe my eyes with my sleeve. "You'd have married someone else."

"Ah, yes." He grimaces. "You're right. But no one else could have brought *Volk Smerti* to heel. I'm in love, and I couldn't be happier. Now, where's my Christmas present?"

I hand him a small box topped with a foil rosette. He opens it and pulls out a set of car keys.

"Oh, you are *shitting* me," he exclaims. "You don't have any money yet. How did you–"

"Fyodor gave me an advance on the money from Pavel's estate. He knows I'm good for it. Let's go and see what's out back, shall we?"

We walk through the kitchen to the patio doors and onto the rear driveway.

According to the brochure, the Aston Martin Vantage is a car for people who love to drive. This one has a V8 engine and hunkers down low over its wheels. The Christmas lights reflect in the metallic red paintwork as they flicker.

Leo turns to me.

"I could have bought one. It was gonna be my gift to myself when I became Pakhan. But you remembered what car I wanted." He shakes his head. "I'm gonna be a kept man. I think I like it."

"Does that mean you gotta do what I say?"

He grins. "Don't get too mouthy, *tigritsa*. I got ways to put you in your place."

I narrow my eyes at him. "That's fighting talk, baby. You wanna duke it out?"

EPILOGUE

Eight months later...

Ali

I miss my parents more than ever today.

My father should be here to walk me down the aisle. But he isn't, so I didn't want an aisle at all. Mama would have loved to help me choose a wedding dress, and I couldn't pick one out without her. So it went, until Leo suggested I stop trying to color inside the lines and just do whatever the hell I wanted.

And here we are. We decided on Hawaii and booked it last minute, so no one could complain they weren't invited.

But we're not alone. I have Roxy, and Leo has Ben. And, of course, we have Luna.

I couldn't deny my little girl a dress, even though I chose to forgo one. She looks like a little princess, but I know it's not gonna last. We have Bowie's greatest hits playing, and already she's bouncing on the bed, playing air guitar.

"Mumma, look! Whooo!"

Leo comes into the room. Luna scrambles to the floor and runs to him, jumping into his arms.

"Hey, Ziggy Stardust," he says. "What's on your hands? You're already a mess." He puts her down, shooing her into the ensuite. "Wash your sticky paws."

Roxy is pinning flowers in my hair. She turns and frowns.

"Ah, it was a chocolate croissant. That's entirely my fault. She said she was hungry, so I gave it to her, but that was *before* we got her dressed. She must have stashed it somewhere like a squirrel."

Leo isn't listening to her. He's looking at me in the mirror.

"You look fucking gorgeous," he says.

I smile, then frown. "Thank you. But watch the cursing around her. You know she's picking it up now."

Leo raises his eyebrows at Roxy. "*You* should know better, young lady."

"Not *me*!" Roxy laughs, punching him in the shoulder. "You look pretty good yourself, Leo. I didn't know you wore anything other than suits and black roll-neck sweaters."

"What's wrong with black?" he asks, stealing a mini bottle of Prosecco from our dressing table. "Good for stealth and hides the blood. At least, that was my logic."

"Am I right in thinking that's all behind you now?" Roxy asks.

"For the time being, yes." He pops the bottle and downs it in one. "But if I'm needed, I'll be there. We owe the *komissiya* a fuck of a lot."

Luna wanders out of the bathroom, shaking her damp hands. "Uckalot!" she cries, her grin just like her father's.

"And I think that's *my* point made," I say. "Go see if the officiant is waiting, and take Her Ladyship with you while we finish up here."

Leo scoops Luna up and puts her on his shoulders, her skirts getting everywhere. She laughs as she pushes the layers of lace over his face.

"I regret this so much already," he says, his voice muffled. He reaches up and pushes the dress out of the way to peals of laughter from Luna.

"Daddy, my bucket!"

"Yep, got it." As they go, he reaches down to pick up the plastic beach bucket from the decking. I watch in the mirror as they head down the patio steps and onto the sand.

It warms my heart to know that Luna won't remember when she didn't have her father. He's spent the last eight months building a relationship with her, and now there are times when I can't get a minute's attention from either of them. She's three years old now and getting bolder and more mischievous every day. One thing is certain - Daddy's girl has him wrapped around her little finger.

Love saved us all.

I'm part of a family again. It's everything I never dared to dream it could be. Today we make it official, but no piece of paper could make this more real than it already is.

I'd die without Leo. Hell, I almost *did*.

The Hawaiian sand is smooth and pale in the early evening light. Luna is piling sand onto her father's feet as he talks to the officiant.

I smile to myself. My little girl has accepted the change in her life with so much grace.

Roxy fixes the last flower in place. "You ready, babe?" she asks.

I stand in front of the mirror and take in the full effect. My ivory lace bodysuit looks luminous against my tanned skin, and the silk wide-legged pants are perfect, soft and billowing around my frame. I wear diamond studs in my ears and, of course, my beloved bracelet.

Roxy has opted for a sundress, but she fretted and fussed for weeks over what to choose. I know why it matters, but she's strangely tight-lipped about it.

"I'm gonna ask you one more time," I say as I pick up my single white rose. "What is your thing with Ben?"

She looks past me, and I see Ben waiting on the beach with Leo.

Roxy looks flustered. "Nothing, and that's the problem. He thinks I'm a kid."

I can't help but laugh. "You don't think he might feel a bit awkward? He shot you in the leg. As meet-cutes go, it's not the best. You just need to stop acting like a teen with a crush and play harder to get."

"What, like *you*?" She narrows her eyes at me, a smirk playing on her lips. "You are *not* qualified to give that lesson."

I shrug, but it's understood that I'm conceding the point. Luna runs up the beach, her hair coming undone in the ocean breeze.

"Daddy says hurry!"

"That's your cue." She gives me a quick hug. "Let's do this thing!"

∽

Roxy was right - Leo is looking pretty good. In fact, I'm struggling to concentrate on the ceremony.

He has *two* wedding presents for me. One of them required me to agree to no sex for a week. I wasn't even allowed to make *myself* come. This has been more than a bit of a challenge, given that we've been here for five days, and Leo has been shirtless about eighty percent of that time. Now he's making linen look damn fine, although I'm so hot for him by now that he could wear *anything* and I'd still be losing my mind with lust. I'd prefer him to wear *nothing*, of course, but that's for later.

A wicked idea occurs to me.

I slip my ring finger along the stem of the rose in my hand, feeling for a thorn. The pad of my fingertip yields at first, but when I press harder, the skin splits, blood running into my palm. I hold the flower at my side, subtly swapping it to the other hand.

The officiant directs Leo to put the ring on my finger. He reaches for me and notices that I'm bleeding.

"Oh!" The officiant looks horrified, the color draining from her cheeks as she sees the injury. "Are you alright?"

Leo doesn't take his eyes off me. I glance to see Ben and Roxy, both looking confused. When I look at Leo again, his eyes are burning into me.

"She's fine," he says. "Carry on."

He slips the ring over my bloodied knuckle, caressing it with his thumb. I shudder at his touch.

He'll make me pay for this little stunt. I have no doubt.

Luna is oblivious, thankfully. She's wandered away to chase a crab, and I smile as I see her catch it under her bucket.

"I'm delighted to pronounce you man and wife." The officiant looks worried, and she's speaking fast. I suspect she thinks we're weird and wants to get this over with. "You may kiss the bride."

Leo clasps my hand for a moment, then releases it to stroke my cheek tenderly as he leans in. His lips are warm, and his tongue invades my mouth as he smears the blood on my face.

"Later, *tigritsa*," he murmurs.

The bar is packed with people like us - happy souls in love. But they're not *really* like us. How could they be?

Roxy went back to her beach lodge an hour ago, taking the sleepy Luna with her. Ben made his excuses shortly after. It'll be cute if they are having a babysitting date right now but I doubt it – he's been guarded and distant all day

It's not the time to get into that. Today is about Leo and me.

We cleaned up after the ceremony, but red spots still blot my pants, and the lines on my palm are still stained red. Leo traces his fingertip over my hand.

"Shall we dance?"

"I thought you'd never ask," I say, putting my drink on the bar. "I thought you'd just *insist*. That's what happened on the night we met."

"That's not *all* that happened." He takes my hand and leads me onto the floor. "I seem to remember *you* wanted to do a lot more than just dance. I just did what I was told."

He takes hold of my waist. I wrap my arms around his neck as we sway to the music.

"This is perfect." I kiss him. "I never imagined happiness like this would ever find me."

"Me neither." He runs a hand through my hair, settling it on the back of my head as he pulls me closer. "I didn't know what a family was. My own father hated me, and Pavel - well, he was worse, in a way."

"How?"

"He let me believe he cared about me, and in return, I'd have done anything for him. But the first and only time I defied him, he went fucking crazy. He didn't just want you dead. He was prepared to make *me* kill you, only to..."

His words die on his lips, and I look up at him. His eyes are dark with anger.

"I can't think about what he would have done to Luna," he says. "It hurts to know I've lost a father figure. But I took my daughter straight to him and almost got her killed. I don't know if I'll ever forgive *myself* for that."

I squeeze his shoulder. "You did the only thing that made sense at the time. How could you have known that Pavel would do what he did?"

We fall silent for a minute. It's tough for Leo to talk about what happened, and a few moments of respectful peace feel like the right response for now. We both need to heal, and we have a lifetime to work on it.

"I'll tell you one thing, *tigritsa*," he says, smiling at me. "I might be a legend, but *you* are right up there with me in the badass stakes. There's no one in the Bratva who hasn't heard the tale of how Pavel Gurin's niece came back from the dead not once, but *twice*."

I shrug. "I suppose not many people will ever burst out of a body bag to shoot someone."

Another couple dancing close by overhear us. The woman's eyes catch mine.

"Don't worry," I say to her. "Neither of has a gun right now."

Leo looks over his shoulder and grins at her. She says nothing, but she blushes, and her partner looks furious.

"Better watch it, buddy," Leo says. "Seems like your woman *wants* a bit of danger in her life."

～

"Are you gonna put me out of my misery?" I ask.

We're back at our beach house. Luna is staying with Roxy overnight so we can have the place to ourselves.

Leo puts a gift box on the table. Beside it is a brown envelope.

"So when does your course finish?" he asks, pouring wine.

"I don't care about that right now, Leo." I pick up my glass and take a sip. The wine is cold and dry, a wonderful relief from the evening's humidity. "I'm much more interested in getting you out of your clothes."

"Too bad." He unbuttons his shirt cuffs, tucking them as he rolls up his sleeves. "I'm asking."

My mouth goes dry, but it's not from the wine. How does he expect me to talk about my day-to-day life when all I can think about is getting my hands on him?

Since we arrived, every woman who set eyes on him did a double take. His skin is burnished, and his dark blonde hair has picked up highlights in the sun, making his sea-green eyes seem even brighter. I've developed a boastful swagger in the last few days, but I can't help it.

This beautiful man is *mine*.

He raises his eyebrows at me. I realize he's not gonna drop the subject.

"Okay, okay," I say. "Roxy will finish before the end of the year. She's got a job at the city orphanage, starting in January. But I'm probably gonna quit my classes."

"No you're not, he frowns. "You want to be there for those kids. Be the person who listens to them, helps them feel safe."

"We've been through this. I have a criminal record, Leo. Outstanding warrants, all sorts. And now I'm in the fucking *Bratva*, so that's not gonna help matters."

"I beg to differ." Leo nudges the brown envelope toward me. "Take a look."

I pull out a cardboard file. On the front is a sticker with the name I gave at random the first time I was arrested – *Alina Green.*

I never thought about it before. After I woke from my coma, I gave my first name, but then I wouldn't speak again. I never even *had* a second name until a police officer demanded one of me, and that's what I chose.

Green. Gurin. So close.

Somewhere deep down, I knew all along.

"That file," Leo says, "contains everything the police have on you."

I open it. It's empty.

"Does this mean what I think it means?"

"Yep." Leo takes my hand, kissing my palm. "As far as the law is concerned, you're nobody. I'm sorry it took so long, but Fyodor needed to move some money around and call in a few favors."

I melt into his arms.

It's not just a clean slate. It's as though the shame and ignominy of my life has been scrubbed away. I can keep the lessons I've learned, but now I have a second chance at a useful life. Little Ali didn't have anybody, and I want to do everything I can to spare other children the suffering I experienced.

"Thank you," I whisper. "I didn't even know it was possible."

Leo kisses the top of my head. "It's *not* possible from a legal standpoint, but let's just say that's there's very little you can't achieve with money and threats." He lets go of me and picks up the gift box, placing it in my hands. "Now, *this* gift could go either way in terms of how happy it makes you, so let's see."

I sit on the couch and put the box on my knees. I remove the lid to reveal something I recognize but have never seen before in real life.

It's a wand. Not the imitation 'massager' type, or even the high-end Lelo brand, but a Hitachi. Old-school, hardcore, mains powered.

"Holy shit," I say. "Knowing you as I do, I have a good idea what you're gonna do with *that*."

Leo grins and takes a big swig of his wine.

"This week has been fucking awful," he says. "Seriously. That bikini of yours. Where's the rest of it? I kept up my side of the bargain, but *Jesus*. I nearly lost my mind."

He walks over to the couch and takes the box from me, setting it on the floor, and kneels.

"This is where I belong," he says. "At your feet, on my knees. You're my wife, and I'll worship you for the rest of my days."

I slide into his lap and kiss him, grinding my hips.

"That's lovely," I murmur, "but I really, *really* need to come. You can help me with that, right?"

"Eventually." Leo pushes me back onto the couch and reaches for my waistband. "But I'm in no hurry."

There's a whisper of silk as he slides my trousers over my skin, and he bites his lip at the sight of me in just the bodysuit.

"What the fuck *is* this thing you're wearing?" he asks, parting my legs.

"You're not the only one who can do surprises, you know."

The bodysuit is open at the crotch, a string of pearls sitting neatly between my pussy lips. The largest pearl presses insistently on my clit, teasing me.

"This has been tucked away in your pants all day?" he asks, his voice hoarse. He leans in close and runs his tongue along the line of pearls, making me quiver. "It must have been driving you crazy. But fuck *me*, does it look sexy."

He kneels up, pressing his hardening cock against my damp sex as he kisses me. I nip his tongue with my teeth.

"You think you can rile me up so I'll give you what you want, don't you?" he asks. "Nuh-uh, *tigritsa*. You're gonna suffer. For strutting around with your gorgeous body on show all week, for making yourself bleed during our wedding ceremony. Don't move."

He pushes the straps of the bodysuit away from my shoulders, kissing my collarbone as he moves down. My nipples pebble in the cool sea air, and his lips feel warm as he teases them. I'm not used to him being so slow and gentle. I tilt my hips, trying to push against him and relieve the ache in my core.

"Fucking stay still," Leo growls. "You're my wife. Do what I tell you."

I try not to squirm as he bites my nipples, his teeth scraping them lightly. My pussy is already throbbing needfully, wanting him to fill it with anything – fingers, cock, tongue, I'll take any and all of what he has for me.

Leo leaves the bodysuit at my waist and sits back on his heels, enjoying the view between my legs. I feel his breath on me, then the tip of his tongue nudging my clit.

He's doing it on purpose. Not getting in there, not giving me relief. My clit sends bolts of pleasure up my spine with each little lick until I forget myself entirely.

"Stop it!" I cry. "Leo, I'm dying here. Will you *please* just—"

Suddenly, his face is inches from mine. He claps a hand over my mouth and leans his weight onto me, pinning me to the couch. I feel two fingers of his other hand part my slick pussy lips, one on each side of the pearls, and I groan into his palm.

Leo's eyes hold me. I can't look away. I gasp as he slides his fingers inside, stretching me.

"That fucking shut you up, didn't it?" he says.

He shifts his thumb to the pearl on my clit, pressing it down. It rolls against my swollen button, and my internal walls clench around his fingers as pleasure seizes my muscles. I want to fight him, but I'm completely powerless. His hand is too strong, and I wriggle as he maintains the pressure over my mouth. My pussy gets ever wetter as he strokes his fingers slowly in and out of me.

Leo's eyes keep sliding away from me. He's looking at the box on the floor, and I know I'm in real trouble. Because I want to come, he knows it, and he's not gonna let me.

I hope against hope that he'll get too lost in what he's doing to execute his diabolical plan, but I should have known better. Just as the heat begins to gather in my abdomen, he breaks eye contact with me, removing his hand from my mouth. My pussy shudders with the loss as he pulls his fingers free.

Before I can say anything, he shoves his fingers into my mouth, rubbing my juice over my tongue. Instinctively, I bite him, and he roars with frustration, gripping my chin and pulling it down so I'm forced to open my jaw. I look at him and laugh.

"You're always gonna fight me, aren't you?" he says, a wicked smirk on his face as he flexes his injured fingers.

"I can't keep it up forever," I say, leaning back on my elbows. "At some point I'll have to give up and do whatever you want, as long as you'll let me come."

Leo grins and reaches for the Hitachi, plugging it into the outlet in the wall. He holds it up, perusing the buttons.

"Ah," he says. "Simple. On, and turn the dial here to increase the intensity." With a click, the wand hums to life, the head quivering.

"I've never used one of those," I say.

"You're not going to." Leo touches the wand to my inner thigh, making me jump. "*I'm* going to use it on *you*. You don't have to worry about whether you'll orgasm, *tigritsa*. You'll come as many times as I want you to. And I won't fuck you until you're an absolute wreck."

"That's cruel."

"What's your point?" He turns off the wand abruptly, putting it down beside him, and reaches for his ankle. "That reminds me. This is for you." He removes his small blade from the ankle holster and sets it down on the couch cushion beside me. "In case you want to get me back for what I'm about to do to you."

"Why the fuck did you have a knife on you?"

"Force of habit." He picks up the Hitachi, turning it on again. "Now let's see how you like this piece of hardware, shall we?"

I've used vibrators, but this thing is in another class entirely. The head of it is the size of a tangerine, and it's not intended for penetration – it's for total clitoral stimulation.

Leo touches the head of the wand to the pearl on my clit. The vibrations are so strong that they spread through my entire pussy, but the pearl shimmies in place, setting my swollen clit alight with sensation. I moan, my mouth falling open.

"Oh, I fucking *love* this thing," Leo says. "I think you like it too. Let's amp it up a bit."

He nudges the dial, and the wand finds another gear, the low hum increasing in pitch as it speeds up. He presses the whole end onto my pussy, grinding it against me, and I'm bowled over by the feeling.

It's so intense that it's almost numbing, but not quite. My clit is throbbing wildly, unable to keep up with the onslaught, and now I understand what it really means to force an orgasm. I've seen it done in porn but never thought it was real – now, my climax is hurtling toward me like a speeding car, and nothing I could do would prevent it from hitting me.

Leo looks spellbound as I convulse before him. My gasps turn into cries, and just as it's about to happen, he plunges his fingers into me once more, pumping them hard as he holds the wand in place.

I scream as I come, my pussy gushing fluid all over the couch and onto Leo. My clit zings with pleasure as the wand stimulates me past my orgasm and into over-sensitivity. I shriek and swat at Leo's hand, and he moves the wand away from me.

My entire body is shaking from the aftershocks. He *made* that happen, and it felt incredible.

Leo seems to read my mind.

"You liked having no say in that." He dips his fingers into the puddle I made, licking his fingers. "And I sure as fuck liked forcing it on you. I'm not a good guy, I guess."

I stare at him through hooded eyes as he switches the wand on again. I know I should say or do *something*, but my legs are jelly and my willpower is nowhere to be found.

If I really wanted to stop him, I would. But I want to see how far he'll take me.

Leo stands and walks to the side of the couch, shedding his clothes as he does so. He gestures at me to lie down lengthways, and I do as I'm bid, smiling up at him. He grasps his erection, tapping it on my chin as he brandishes the wand like a sword.

"I'm gonna make you come again," he says, rubbing the smooth head on my lips as he speaks. "Just turn sideways and keep your slutty mouth wide open. Understand?"

I nod and open my mouth.

"That's my good girl."

Leo thrusts his cock into my throat, bottoming out immediately, and I gag hard. He holds my head in place with his free hand as he presses the head of the Hitachi against my pussy again.

My nerves are completely fried. The super-strong vibrations hit me for the second time, and it's as though I'm already sprinting for the finish. My clit throbs in agony, but the stimulation pushes me past the pain and hijacks my body, sending powerful waves of ecstasy through my core. My pussy clenches, and so does my throat, drawing a low moan from Leo.

"You gonna come again?" he murmurs, sounding awestruck. "Fucking *yes*. Do it."

He grips my head, holding me still so he can fuck my mouth hard as I orgasm. I scream around his shaft as he ravages my throat, the wand still shuddering relentlessly against my quivering sex. He moves it away, pulling his cock from my mouth as he does so. I draw a deep, gasping breath, panting hard as I look up at him.

"If I fuck you now, you might die," Leo says, jerking off idly over my face.

"Only if *I* fucking kill you!"

He looks so incredibly sexy. He's looming over me, his erection huge and wet with my saliva as he strokes it. No one in the world but me will ever see him this way, and I feel pretty damn good about it.

"I think I gotta get at it from behind, Ali," he says, hauling me to my feet. My legs almost give way, but he holds me upright long enough to turn me around and push me onto all fours on the couch. "Can I trust you with that wand? I want another one from you before we're done."

"I can't come again," I say, my voice cracking a little as his cock nudges my dripping pussy, making me instantly regret my words.

Of *course* I can come again. If my husband wishes it so, it's gonna happen.

Leo takes the little blade and carefully cuts the string of pearls off my bodysuit, throwing them on the floor. He passes the wand to me, putting it in my right hand. In my left, he puts the knife.

"Leo, I—"

"Just don't get them mixed up," he says. "Tell me when you're gonna come and I'll flip you over, baby. You can get your revenge on me then."

I sigh as he sinks his cock into me. My pussy is supple and wet from my orgasms, but he still fills me completely, stretching me to accommodate him. I angle the wand beneath me and turn it on, jumping as it makes contact with my body.

"Fuck," Leo says, grabbing my ass with both hands, "I can feel that. I'm too far gone now, but next time I'm gonna find a way to get in on that action."

He leans on me, his weight pressing him deeper. The very tip of him hits the spot deep inside, pushing a throb of pleasure through my body.

He pulls out of me completely, and I'm about to protest when he shoves his cock back into my pussy, thrusting his thumb into my asshole simultaneously.

There's so much to feel. Everything hurts, but it's so fucking good at the same time. I drop my head into the pillow as Leo thrusts harder, his free hand holding my hair.

"You gotta tell me when!" he cries.

"Any second!" I manage to gasp, dropping the wand on the floor. He wrenches his cock out of my clinging cunt and pulls his thumb out of my ass, flipping me over with a swat of his hand. I scream as he pulls my legs apart, plunging back inside me.

"I'm gonna fuck you through it," he says, taking hold of my neck. "You know what I need, don't you?"

I still have the knife in my other hand. As he presses on my throat, I raise the blade to his chest, touching it to the ear of his wolf tattoo.

He knows I'm gonna do it, but I wait until my pussy starts convulsing around his cock. He fucks me harder, his eyes fixed on mine.

"Do it," he says, his breath hot in my face. "I want it baby, come on—"

At the peak of my pleasure, I tilt the knife, the sharp edge cutting his skin. It's not deep, but it's a keen, long slice, and the blood appears immediately, dripping onto my breasts. I toss the knife aside and with a roar, Leo slams me hard and comes inside me, adding to the wetness and heat of my pussy.

We're still for a minute, him pinning me to the couch with his bulk. Then I feel the chill in the air, and push him off me.

The cut to his chest looks a little worse now that there's blood everywhere. He looks down at it and grins.

"You've fucking trashed my tattoo," he says. "Six hours I sat getting this done. But when it heals, I think I'll like the scar even more."

∿

"Do you think we'll ever be one of those Hallmark couples?" I ask as I emerge from the ensuite, robe in hand.

I smile as I see Leo on the decking, wine glass in hand. He's buck naked in the breeze, gazing up at the stars.

"Did you say something, beautiful wife?"

I pull the robe over my body and join him outside. "I was just asking whether we're gonna end up settling down and becoming one of those couples from the movies."

"If the movie in question is pay-per-view, then maybe."

"I mean the rom-com types, you know." I smile as he frowns at me. "The ones who do stuff like baking and ice-skating and have polite sex in never more than three positions."

"No fucking way, *tigritsa*." He puts an arm around my shoulder. "One day we might make beautiful love as an orchestral theme plays, but until then, I'm honored to bleed for you, live for you, and love you always. And rail you every which way, obviously."

I can't help but laugh.

I never knew how much space in my heart was taken up with pain. Now that I have my husband — my *family* — my heart is full of *them*. There's no place for anything that can hurt me, unless it's Leo, only hurting me in all the best ways.

"I love you," I say. "You didn't just *not* kill me. You *saved* me, and gave me something to live for."

"Not before *you* saved *me*," he replies. "And as for not killing you, well, there's time yet. We're married now, aren't we supposed to fight all the time?"

"I hope so."

He chuckles as he pulls me in for a kiss.

"I love you too."

THE END

Thanks for reading!

If you enjoyed **Twisted Sinner**, you may also be interested in reading **Depraved Royals**, which is Kal and Dani's story. Read FREE in Kindle Unlimited or buy on Amazon at the link below:

Depraved Royals

MAILING LIST

Thanks for reading! Reviews are appreciated. I hope you enjoyed this book!

Sign up to my mailing list and get bonuses, freebies and offers emailed straight to your inbox.

Sign up at this link:

http://eepurl.com/h7lpFb

ALSO BY CARA BIANCHI

Thanks for reading!

If you enjoyed **Twisted Sinner**, you may also be interested in reading **Depraved Royals**, which is Kal and Dani's story. Read FREE in Kindle Unlimited or buy on Amazon at the link below:

Depraved Royals

Also by Cara Bianchi:

Tainted Vow

Santori Mafia:

Bound to the Devil

Stolen by the Killer